Never Do Harm

To Bob
best wishes.

Never Do Harm

Mirren Jones

E. M. Atkins
Marian C. Duffy

Mirren Jones is the pseudonym of the collaborative writing partnership of Marion Duffy and Elaine Atkins.

Never Do Harm is their second novel.

Visit their website: www.mirrenjones.co.uk

Also by these authors

Fiction

Eight of Cups

Non-fiction

Facilitating Groups in Primary Care

Facilitating Organisational Change in Primary Care

Praise for Eight of Cups

'A compelling debut novel'

The Scots Magazine

'This is an excellent first novel . . . a genuine page-turner. It's acutely responsive to contemporary mainstream realism, ranging from sharp exposition and informationally rich language, to crisp dialogue, replete with far-flung geographies.'

Dr Simon Jenner, Royal Literary Fund Fellow

'A bittersweet story, rooted in familiar Scottish settings, which both entertains and challenges all readers to stop and think about their own attachments.'

Anthony Troon, Columnist

This novel is a work of fiction. The characters and their names are the work of the authors' imaginations. Any resemblance to actual persons, living or dead, is coincidental.

A catalogue record for this record is available

from the British Library.

ISBN 978-0-9560841-5-6

E-book ISBN 978-0-9560841-3-2

First published in Great Britain 2018 by EM People, Crathie Bridge, Meigle, Blairgowrie, Perthshire, PH12 8QZ

Cover image 'Titania'

by kind permission of sculptor Christine Baxter

http://www.chrisbaxtersculptor.co.uk

Dedicated to our friends and colleagues
in the NHS

and in memory of

Dr Andrew Martin
and
Mr Malcolm Clayton

Médicins Sans Frontières

Marseille 2012

It's an everyday situation for her.

A bar.

A man.

A drink.

Again and again until demand, or luck, runs out.

Today it's the same bar as yesterday. Bar Caravelle on Rue de la Partigon. Nothing fancy. And it's the same drink as yesterday too – vodka, with just a splash of water. It warms her up, and after a few glasses she begins to feel numb, and that's good, it helps with whatever follows. But the man sitting opposite her is not the usual punter in this part of the city.

Would you like another drink, miss? He speaks

French with an educated accent.

Yes, thanks.

She had already noticed, as he poured the first glass, that his hands were clean and soft, not the hands of a Marseille labourer. Gentle hands? Perhaps, but not likely. When was the last time she had such hands on her?

She has been snatching furtive glances at him, avoiding eye contact. She estimates he's in his late fifties. His hands may be young but his face and neck are deeply lined. His shoulders are hunched; he has a look of weariness about him. Good – then it won't take long.

She never feels pity for any of them, the saddos – why should she? But yet, perhaps a twinge for this one; he's carrying some weight on those shoulders for sure, and he was probably handsome at one time.

They drink again, fast, not conversing.

Shall we go? she asks. Time is money, after all, and they've been there a good half an hour.

He nods his head in agreement, picks up his jacket from the chair-back and follows her out into the darkening street.

The room is sparsely furnished, but clean, with a washbasin in the corner. She is business-like as normal. Asks him what he wants, explains the cost of 'extras'.

Just undress, he says, your bottom half only, lie on the bed and wait for me.

He washes his hands methodically, in the way he's done a thousand times before, rubbing the soap all over the palms and backs, and between his fingers, letting the water flow over them until the soap has disappeared. He dries them on the towel next to the sink. His back is still to her. She doesn't see him pull a surgical glove out of his pocket and onto his left hand.

Lift your knees up, keep your feet together, he commands softly. This won't take long.

She complies, although she's growing more uneasy by the minute. This is a strange request, why isn't he getting his prick out?

Your trousers, she asks. Are you going to take them off?

He appears not to have heard her. Moving to her hip, he says in a quiet voice, Now, open your knees for me and relax. This won't hurt.

His left hand slides up into her and his right presses down on her thin, white, belly, palpating it firmly.

Stop it you freak! She attempts initially to pull away but they're locked up like dogs mating and she'll hurt herself if she continues to struggle.

He says nothing, simply withdraws his hand, pulls off the glove, walks to the waste basket and drops it in.

She pulls her skirt on frantically, as fast as her shaking arms will allow.

Get out! I don't want your money. Just go. Now!

As if she doesn't exist, he walks slowly to the door, and leaves, not bothering to close it on the way out.

Shaken, but not so badly that she can't rush after him, she shuts the door firmly and slips the bolt. Leaning against the door she breathes shallow and fast, adrenaline flooding her body.

Another fucking weirdo. Why me?

She slumps heavily onto the bed, rubs her hands over her face and pushes her hair back over her head, then presses her fingers against her eyeballs in an effort to stem the tears that have welled up in her eyes.

She really can't stand this job much longer. That's an hour gone already and nothing to show for it except an ache between her legs. She must get back to work. Walk the street again, find another man, a normal one this time. Ten minutes, give her the money and go.

Beware the effects of alcohol

Edinburgh 1975

A couple of weeks before the end of the spring term, Hugh was sitting with his legs hanging over the arm of the battered leather armchair in Alan's room in Mylne's Court, reading the Sunday Post and quoting fictional but almost credible, 'Letters to the Hon Man'.

'Hugh, will you shut up for a minute. I've just had a thought,' said Alan.

'Well, don't stress yourself out about it,' said Hugh, straining his neck to check his appearance in the mirror behind Alan's desk. 'You've got exams soon.'

'Very funny. Ha, ha. Stop admiring yourself in that mirror and pay attention to me, you vain bastard. I was thinking – when you're down in Rennes on that rugby trip, you're not too far from Dinan.'

'Mmm. Where a certain gypsy lady resides maybe?'

Alan pointed his finger at Hugh.

'Look – you'll have to stop calling her that. It was just her father who came from Romany stock. And he's long gone. She's perfectly normal and civilised like you and me. Well, me anyway. Now, what I was going to say was, if you're actually listening instead of playing Narcissus, would you do me a big favour while you're in the area and be a courier for this precious gift I've got her for her birthday.'

'Whoa! I'll smoke it but I'm not dealing in it! Too risky, man.'

'Don't be bloody daft – it's my granny's necklace – just I wouldn't want it getting lost in the post.'

'Ok. It's possible, possible. Let's get the maps out.'

Having cleared away the empties and the chip papers from the previous night, the two friends began to plan the journey, sitting at Alan's desk in his turret bedroom, with its stunning views over Princes Street and beyond to a misty river Forth.

'Now remember, she's mine,' said Alan. 'Don't you be working your fatal charm on her in my absence. Mind you, I shouldn't really worry. She doesn't like skinny dreeps – or so she told me. She prefers cuddly, strong Scotsmen like me.'

'Oh so she speaks Scots does she?' Hugh retorted.

'I'm teaching her. And she's teaching *me* a few

French words even *I've* never heard of.'

'I bet she is, you lucky boy! Naw, naw. No need to worry. I go for blondes as you well know. Although if Lizzie doesn't drop them soon I might reconsider my position. That's been four bloody weeks now.'

Alan stumbled over a stack of medical textbooks in order to reach the lower drawer of the bedside chest, from where he took a rectangular cream leather jewellery case. He opened it to show Hugh his French Grandmother's gold chain with a delicate filigree drop holding a single ruby. There was a small handwritten card underneath which said, *Je vais tous aime toujours, Alain.*

'Verrrry nice.' Hugh gave a long low whistle.

Alan snapped the lid shut and held out the box to Hugh. 'Now keep it safe. Don't you dare lose it, whatever you do.'

Hugh tucked it deep into his jacket pocket, replying, 'no sweat mate, I won't let you down. A couple of pints in Ensign Ewart's will absolutely guarantee it.'

The University Rugby Club gave Hugh and his rowdy team-mates the usual send-off, a huge booze-up with massive hangovers to nurse on the bus journey to Rennes. Many of the unshaven, tousle-haired lads slept most of the way to the south coast ferry.

The players always lodged with French families who served up wonderful local dishes washed down with wines of variable quality. The Scots' play on the pitch deteriorated directly in line with the volume of wine consumed. The inter-university tour progressed as planned with days two and four designated for 'sightseeing and cultural experiences' – also known as recovery time.

Mike Jackson (prop forward) and Frankie Baxter (fly half) had promised to make the trip to Dinan with Hugh, with a bet on who would pull the first mademoiselle. Nevertheless, when the time came to board the local bus, they were still flat out, snoring blissfully and loudly, chez Mme Le Carpentier.

Hugh himself dozed much of the forty mile circuitous journey, missing local sights and the pleasant undulating countryside.

Having given himself plenty of time before meeting Simone, he wandered round the ancient walled area, with its tabacs, patisseries, cafés and small restaurants. The shops were already closing up for the afternoon *siesta*. Close to the ramparts, he found the small Hotel de la Porte Saint Malo, constructed out of five old stone houses. The entrance was marked by hanging baskets filled with pink and lilac flowers.

He checked again that the box was in his pocket and took another quick look at Alan's photo of Simone smiling to the camera, before slipping through the side door of the hotel. Taking a minute to adjust his eyes to the lack of light, he then followed an arrow round to the right which took him to the reception desk. Judging by the tone of voice, a tall upright elderly German was remonstrating over his bill. Simone, for surely it was her, remained calm, smiled, and patted the old man's arm. It seemed to work.

She caught Hugh's eye, grinned and mouthed '*A bientot'* – soon.

Ten minutes later, she hung up her white apron, blew a kiss to Georges the porter and took Hugh by the arm. 'Allons. I know a good place.'

In *Crêperie des Artisans* on Rue du Petit Fort, once they'd negotiated which language they would use, and aided by a generous litre of house red, they began to relax.

'So the other boys are too ill to come today? Ah, you Scottish! You drink too much. Beaucoup de whisky. No wonder we can defeat you in rugby!' Her eyes sparkled, her voice teased.

'Never! What about les Francais? You drink wine all day. And smoke those horrible Gaulois.'

It was an easy banter which flowed back and forth.

Alan quickly became the focus of the chat.

'Ah my Alain. My big strong Scotsman. How is he now? I miss him so much.'

'He's a great guy you know. And he misses you too. He shows your photograph to everyone and never stops talking about you.'

'Does he have other girls in Scotland?'

'Of course not.'

Hugh placed his hand on his heart. 'You are definitely the only one for him.'

Hugh entertained her with tales of Alan as a boy (always small and stocky, with a petted lip), Alan at secondary school (too slow for rugby, but brilliant at languages), Alan on the golf course (dogged and determined) and Alan the friend (reliable and loyal). She squealed with delight at the old photographs Hugh had brought. The woolly jumpers, the school cap, the scout uniform. Alan as a young boy, Alan as a teenager, Alan rebelling in a very minor way with long hair and droopy moustache.

'And what about you, gypsy girl? Were you a girl guide or a naughty girl at school?'

'Ah Hugh. I always keep these closed' – she gestured to her lips. 'But maybe I can show you some photographs too. Would you like to come to my place for some more coffee?'

Her tiny apartment off Rue de Vergeres was a ten minute stroll from the restaurant. The streets were quiet, doors and windows closed, cats asleep on windowsills.

Simone fussed around with little floral patterned

coffee cups, trying to find matching saucers. Looking for sugar in the cupboard in the corner, she stood on tiptoes, stretching her five feet two inches to its maximum so as to reach the top shelf, exposing a glimpse of smooth olive skin beneath her white cotton blouse.

Hugh had time to study her, the way she moved, cat-like and graceful. Her petite and lithe body. The mass of untamed dark curls now escaping from her hair band, as she shed her receptionist demeanour like a second skin.

The small flat was cluttered, with art magazines piled on the floor, long necklaces hung over the corners of the black mirrored armoire, vintage handbags arranged on a long shelf over her bed and a make-up mirror surrounded by mini pots and brushes on top of the white painted chest of drawers.

He visualised Alan and the gypsy girl making love on that narrow iron-framed bed with its patchwork counterpane. And in an instant he knew.

Just this once. That's all. Just this once.

The coffee was strong and bitter.

'You like it, Hugh? Or maybe better with a cognac?'

He tried hard to focus on the words and not the full-lipped mouth with its very white and perfectly aligned teeth. Framed an image of what that mouth could do. Of the pleasure it might bring.

'When in France, I suppose. Let's have a cognac then. Where are the photographs? Or have you changed your mind?' he teased.

She selected some to show him, laughing to herself at the memories they revived, or occasionally holding one to her chest before passing it over. Studying each one closely, his eyes sought to capture every detail of her. The sidelong glance from under a heavy fringe, unintentionally provocative in a ten year old; the tanned bare legs skipping along the beach in summer shorts; the hint of breast in the thirteen year old schoolgirl; the coy teenage smile from the sunbed. She wasn't classically beautiful, but the little imperfections – a slightly prominent nose, a crooked little finger where she'd fallen running to catch a beautiful butterfly, and the cat shaped birthmark on the inside of her right forearm – only enhanced her appeal.

The last photograph she handed over was a family picture taken on the occasion of her first communion. 'We didn't see too much of my grandparents, you know. It was a very bad thing my Mother did. Bringing shame on the family. My first communion was one of the few times we all celebrated as a big family. My aunts Cecile and Marie with their husbands and children, my Uncle Philippe and his horrible wife Lisette, Grandpère and Grandmère. It was a lovely day.'

'Ah grandmère! Mon dieu! I forgot! I have something for you. From Alan.'

Hugh fumbled in his shirt pocket for the box.

'Close your eyes. And stand very still,' he instructed.

'What is it, what is it? Let me see!'

'No, just wait.'

Standing behind her, he carefully encircled her smooth neck with the chain, positioning the drop so that it lay exactly in the line of her cleavage.

'Now you can look.'

She opened her eyes. Ran to the mirror. Fell silent as she examined the gift, turning this way and that so that the ruby caught the rays of the sun.

'It is so beautiful. I love it. You like it Hugh?'

'I like it very much. There's just one thing I need to do.'

He moved to the mirror and reaching round her shoulders, opened just one small button of her blouse in order to expose the full beauty of the piece.

As she turned to face him, he picked up her arm and softly kissed the dark brown cat shape.

'There. You make it truly beautiful, little gypsy kitten.'

They kissed slowly, savouring the new tastes and smells. He led her across the room, still with his mouth firmly pressed to hers, guiding her backwards on to the beckoning divan.

She tried to say 'we shouldn't.'

'Shh', murmured Hugh. 'Shh.'

And when he undid the remainder of the buttons on her delicate white blouse, she gave up any semblance of a fight and gasped with pleasure as his fingers traced the outline of her small, dark and firm nipples.

She began to rise rhythmically against him, pressing her slim hips into him, arching her back. He moved so that she could feel the full force of his desire for her, so that her ear was pressed against his racing heart.

Her breathing became increasingly rapid and erratic. He tried to slow his down, keep control for a few seconds longer.

As Hugh slid off her soft, moist body, and rolled on to his back, panting and sweating, he shook his head slowly from side to side, as if in disbelief.

Turning back towards her, he said, ' God, Simone, I don't know how that happened. Alan should have warned me just how irresistible you are.'

'Hush. It's over now,' she said, rising quickly and putting a finger to his lips. 'Promise me that Alain will never know. Never!

'Now go. Please. Just go.' She tied the belt of her

bathrobe tightly around herself, as if already punishing her body.

He dressed quickly and left with only a whispered 'I'm sorry,' as she vigorously straightened the bottom sheet and folded her clothes on the chair.

Genetic Predisposition

Dinan 1975

Simone closed the door on Hugh and walked back down the hallway to the kitchen. There were hastily left drinks on the worktop – a vivid reminder. She washed the dirty glasses, wrung the dishcloth out tightly and placed it over the tap to dry. The dull, throbbing pain in her temples was now worsening, spreading over her eyes and around the back of her head; she couldn't ignore it a moment longer. She had to abandon the newly-lit cigarette to reach for aspirins. Sitting down at the table, Simone nursed her head, rubbing her temples in a vain attempt to blot out the pain and the thousand thoughts that filled her mind.

It had been the drink, that's all. A rash few hours, nothing more. And as if she needed to convince herself even further – *Forget it now and move on. It won't change anything. It meant nothing, nothing.* Yet her unsettled stomach was still churning even as she spoke and showed no sign of calming.

Glancing up, she caught sight of herself in the mirror and was disturbed at her reflection – her face appeared worried, tired. *Damn drink! Demon drink! I shouldn't have. Look at me! No more.*

Not for the first time in her life did she remember all the promises to her mother she'd made as a girl.

"I won't touch it! I won't!" Truly she'd meant it at the time. She'd held each word close as she'd spoken, wringing every last drop of honesty out of herself. "I *promise* you Maman. You can trust me." And she'd believed that somehow these pledges would magically save her from turning into a carbon copy of her mother one day – that cognac-soaked pitiful woman, old before her time, her beauty ruined by years of hard drinking.

Simone squeezed her eyes tightly, and there they were again - painful images as if it were only yesterday. The shaking hands grasping the bottle, lifting it just high enough to pour the golden contents into a glass. Her mother's lips opening, the glass draining into the waiting mouth, the cognac disappearing - oh so quickly. Then the shuddering, only to see her reach for the bottle once more, less than a minute later. A videotape jammed on play, rewind, play rewind, over and over again, until she slumped in a stupor. Sometimes on to the table, more often than not on to the floor next to it. Simone developed a dread of arriving home from school. It wasn't a matter of what she would find, but where she might find it, and then how much effort it would take to move her mother's body onto the bed. Despite Yvette's thinness, when drunk she was a dead weight; uncooperative, awkward to balance in Simone's scrawny little arms; yet somehow Simone always managed, except for that very last time. She'd been too frightened to move Maman, with her face so white, white as a sheet. Maman with all that blood on her face and arms. All that blood lying in pools on the floor. All that . . .

The memories were much too distressing. She had to distract herself. She would take a shower immediately; get rid of the smell of sex from her body, and wash away the unfamiliar scent that lingered on her skin. A shower, yes, the feel of water raining down on her body would do.

The water blasted onto her head, flowing over her body as she scrubbed away hard with a sponge in a circular motion, following the contours of her neck, arms, breasts and belly, lathering as she went. She slowed her action down to wash carefully between her legs, surprising herself when she thought briefly of Hugh and immediately felt an involuntary ripple of pleasure surging upwards.

Stop. Enough. Do legs, feet, quickly. Hair next. Shampoo, rinse.

And then cold water to finish, as always, to tone her skin, to wake herself up.

And so it was done. She had washed Hugh out of her hair, off her skin, and from inside her body. There wasn't a trace of him left. Now she could feel pure again.

She dried herself slowly, methodically, with tenderness, in sharp contrast to the roughness of her ablutions. Then she donned a white bathrobe and padded over to the dressing table to sit in front of the mirror.

She pulled herself upright, flicked her hair over her shoulders, looked straight ahead and smiled. A long, slow, closed-lip smile; one meant to reassure. But disappointingly, everything was not quite as it should be, and that uneasiness in her stomach was still present. Perhaps a slight show of teeth would be better? She tried it, peeled her plump lips back to show just a touch of brilliant whiteness.

Yes, that was much better. A smile of confidence. A winning smile. She knew she could improve on it even further with practice. Until it looked completely natural. So that no-one, not even Alain, would suspect otherwise.

Results as expected

Edinburgh 2004

Hugh was singing an old Sinatra classic as he bounded up the stairs. 'And life gets more exciting with each passing day . . . For as rich as you are it's much better to be young at heart ...'

He stopped as he opened the mirrored right hand door of the built-in wardrobe and turned to his wife. 'The grey striped or the blue spotted? Or how about the Bart Simpson the kids bought me for Christmas?'

'Well, Mr Scott, celebrated senior consultant, bon viveur and husband of the year, is it fame or fun we're projecting today?' Anne enquired as she straightened the aqua silk bed cover and plumped up the pillows. 'I'd go for the grey striped tie, Hugh. This is not just a birthday bash remember. You really ought to look the part today in view of your new position.'

'Okay, don't remind me. But once we get the congratulations and hoo-haa over, I aim to kick back and have a bit of serious fun. So see if you can edge the oldies out the door early, will you dearest? I might be fifty now but I'm still *young at heart, yes young at heart.* And I don't want The Major cramping my style. Or your mother getting tipsy on the tiramisu.' He performed a gross caricature of Jane Fotheringham staggering and stumbling around the bedroom, glass in hand, pinkie raised.

'Oh, stop it Hugh. Come on. Let my parents have their day too. Let them bask in the reflected glow of your limelight. Don't forget how their help got you off to a flying start.'

'Will I *ever* be allowed to forget it, I wonder? Anyway, I'm only teasing. So lighten up Anne. Fortunately my lot won't stay long once they've eaten. You know what Father's like about driving in the dark. You'd think the road from Edinburgh to Glasgow crossed the Gobi desert, featureless and frightening.'

He went off to check the temperature of the champagne, still trying (and failing) to sing like Ole Blue Eyes. Anne fastened her gold link bracelet round her slim wrist and gave her face one last quick examination in the make-up mirror, frowning at the discovery of a small brownish age spot on her right cheek.

She'd be fifty herself in July 2006. Just over eighteen months away.

Others thought she had everything – looks, money,

good health, comfortable lifestyle, happy family and devoted husband.

With a long, drawn-out sigh, followed by a deep in-breath and straightening of the shoulders, Anne shut the bedroom door and adopted a welcoming smile.

Cammy and Liz, and Duncan and Lorna arrived first, neighbours on either side of them in Murrayfield Gardens. Liz in Paul Costelloe, befitting an Edinburgh Stockbroker's wife, and Lorna in a ruby velvet Biba dress from Armstrongs in the Grassmarket, just voted number six in the Independent's Top 50 UK Vintage Shops.

Duncan's green velvet smoking jacket was simply old and well loved.

Lorna couldn't resist giving the Rennie Mackintosh inspired nameplate a rub with her sleeve as Hugh opened the stained glass inner door.

'Didn't know what to get you old boy, but thought this might come in handy for the away games in Paris!' jested the balding New Town lawyer as he handed over an awkwardly wrapped gift.

The portable urinal held a bottle of 14 year old Cragganmore.

'Very funny, Duncan. Who's got a dipstick so I can test the contents for sugar?

'And I suppose **this** is a packet of incontinence pads

to go with it?' Hugh joked as he took a squashy package out of the silver gift bag.

The new Glasgow Accies' FP sweatshirt.

In mock offence he added, 'Large? Who are you kidding? I can still fit in to my old school blazer I'll have you know. Thanks Cammy, it's great. I love it. You too Liz. Okay, enough of the jokes. Help yourselves to a glass of champers from the tray and head for the sitting room. My beautiful wife will be with you in a minute.'

The bow-fronted, high-ceilinged room, newly decorated in subtle tones of cream and taupe, was easily large enough for the 40 or so friends and family who slowly filled it over the next hour, as the sun dipped below the horizon and left a cold blue-grey gloaming behind it. A November Sunday in Edinburgh's genteel west end.

Major and Mrs Fotheringham settled themselves on the squashy brown leather sofas alongside Andrew and Muriel Scott, admiring the latest studio portraits of their shared grandchildren Emily and Andrew, currently broadening their minds in a bar in the Ko San Road in Bangkok.

'What is this gap year business all about anyway? Never heard of it in our day. Conscription would be a better idea.'

Jane Fotheringham exchanged a wearied look with

Muriel Scott. That same old refrain from the same old boring husbands.

'Oh just ignore him. He's like a broken down record. Who's this coming up the drive now?'

The Edinburgh Royal Hospital Gynaecology and Obstetrics Department contingent, arriving almost en masse, gravitated one by one towards the kitchen where every conceivable drink option was available, with a lead crystal glass to suit and a willing pourer on hand. Junior Consultant Robin Gray waved away Finlay Scott's offer of a whisky. 'Unfortunately I'm on call. Someone has to do it. Make mine a diet Coke please.' The others were obviously travelling home by taxi.

Old 'Beaky' Brown, Hugh's mentor for many years, picked up a stray medical journal and peered at it over the top of his half-moons. 'Hugh? I heard a rumour at the club that you were going to be editing this erstwhile publication. I hope you told them I taught you everything you know?'

'I'm just waiting for my old friend Alan Fraser and his wife Simone to arrive and then I'll tell you all about it, Beaky.'

Alan, running late after a game of golf, was parking his black 4 X 4 in a nearby street, admiring the solid elegance of the Victorian terrace.

'We could have been living in a street like this too, Simone, if *we'd* had a leg up from the parents when *we* got married.'

'And, if you were now swanning about as a top consultant instead of being a hardworking GP. But don't begrudge Hugh his success, my darling. He's worked hard for it. Anyway, I like our house better. It's quirky and interesting, and it's home, not a show house. Don't you agree Luc?'

'What? Can't hear you.'

'Take those damn headphones out right now and look lively, boy. It's your Uncle Hugh's day and you can at least pay attention to what's going on.' Alan straightened the boy's collar as he spoke. Luc squirmed and wriggled out of his grasp. Simone raised her eyes to the skies behind Alan's back and mouthed, 'not today, Luc, please.'

Hugh's strategy had been well thought out. He'd have a couple of gins before everyone arrived, make a bit of an exhibition of himself announcing his good news and then ensure everyone had plenty to drink until the atmosphere lightened, the noise swelled and, hastening the oldies out of the door, the ties could come off. Then it would be *game on*.

With a piercing whistle Hugh gained the attention of the guests. 'Oyez! Oyez! Oyez! Ladies and gentlemen. A word from your host. Gather round and make sure your glass is charged. My wee brother Finlay (pointing to the younger man in blue jeans and a white collarless shirt wielding the champagne bottle) will top up your glass if it's empty.

'I will now a say a few words.'

Hugh, with Anne by his side brushing a stray grey hair from his shoulder, addressed the gathering.

'As you all know, or might have guessed by now, I have reached the age of great wisdom and maturity.' Cue guffaws and whistles.

'I would like to thank you all for joining us here today to celebrate. I will then immediately revert to a suave and intellectual forty-nine year old.'

'Get on with it!'

'Besides the big five-0, I have one more cause for celebration today. It has been a poorly kept secret that The Royal College of Obstetricians and Gynaecologists of which I am a Fellow – all bow before me – has appointed me as editor of their esteemed publication JCOG, otherwise known as the International Journal of Obstetrics and Gynaecology.'

'Give the man a coconut!'

'You will be pleased to know that this honour will not change me in any way. I'll still be the same insufferable smug so-and-so you've always known. However, I would like to thank all those who've provided a helping hand in my rise to fame – Mum and Dad for passing on the genes for excellence, Beaky Brown for giving me plenty of opportunity to study the female nether regions (purely for educational purposes of course) and my colleagues past and present at Edinburgh Royal among whose miserable ranks I continue to shine like a beacon!'

'Get him off!'

'Seriously folks. I appreciate all the help and support you've given me over the years. Now, just before we crack open a few more bottles and get tucked in to Anne's lovely food, I want to acknowledge the role played by my beautiful wife. Her John Lewis bills have kept me hard at work and no doubt will continue to do so.'

Anne feigned outrage.

'To Anne and Hugh.'

'Hugh and Anne.'

'Anne and Hugh.'

Plenty cheering, whistling and laughing to drown out Anne's reply of, 'You are one incorrigible bastard, Hugh.'

'Ah my dear buttoned-up wife. Don't you worry. They all know it's just a joke. Now smile sweetly and mingle. There's Simone over by the window. She won't know anyone here. I'm off to catch up with Alan.'

'Alan, my old mucker.' Hugh slapped him on the back. 'Thanks for coming along to add a note of gravitas to these proceedings. It's been a while. How're you doing out in the Styx?'

'All the better for still being forty nine, my aged

friend, although to tell you the truth, I feel ninety some days. New GP contract or not. And Musselburgh is hardly the Styx, although on a Saturday night outside the Co-op it often feels like it. The load at work never seems to get much lighter, what with all this QOF business.' Alan drew back from giving a tale of woe, as he lightened his tone and jokingly poked his friend in the chest. 'Talking of which – you must be due for a blood pressure check! Phone up my receptionist and make an appointment will you? I wouldn't like to miss out on valuable points because some old senior consultant is too busy golfing to come in and see his GP! '

'Bloody GPs. Gatekeepers to the health service on one hand, and hauling them in off the streets with the other to make a few extra bucks. You should have stuck in at surgery and you could have been like me now – King of the Bloody Castle.'

Alan deflected the cynical dig. 'Enough! Enough! How're the kids? I expected to see them here but the Major tells me they're away on a gap year. He didn't seem impressed.'

'Well, he wouldn't, would he? Reactionary old Tory. They're apparently fine, or so they say in their sporadic emails home.

'It's what they don't say that worries me, and Anne of course scours any photos for evidence of not eating properly, getting too much sun or mixing with shady characters. Fortunately they're travelling together and sticking to the well-worn traveller routes.'

'Is that round the world by a thousand bars, bunjee jumps and elephant rides?'

'Something like that. Today it's Bangkok, then Koh Samui, and up to Chang Mai. They go on to Australia in a couple of weeks, New Zealand and back via Los Angeles in time for New Year. Bank of Mum and Dad paying of course. That's the trouble with sending them to these posh private schools. The children must go travelling daahling. I should have bought shares in Trailfinders.'

Alan shook his head and sighed.

'Changed days. The furthest I got was a year's exchange to France, working in that hospital in Brittany. I was so hard up I survived on bread and cheese. And the odd glass of red. You remember that wee flat Simone had? No – you wouldn't have seen it when you were there that time. She'd make a meal out of leftovers from the hotel that were supposed to go in the pig bin.'

Now it was Hugh's turn to steer the conversation in another direction. 'Talking of Simone, we'd better go in and find the girls. And I need to circulate a bit more. Go and get yourself a drink and chill out for a while. The fun'll start once the parents and the in-laws go home.'

'Anne. You're looking amazing. It must be that old husband of yours keeping you sweet.' Alan embraced her with genuine affection, pulling her in tightly to his chest.

'You're not so bad yourself Alan. It's lovely to see you both. And I spotted Luc earlier. He's chatting with Finlay near the fireplace, no doubt a trip down the Zambezi or a trek across the Serengeti in the planning. He's grown much taller since we last saw him. Must have been a couple of years ago was it?'

Alan's attention had been grabbed by the sound of Simone squealing as Hugh made to swing her up in his arms.

'Hugh, Hugh. Stop it you mad boy! Act your age!'

Hugh feigned an old man's stumbling gait and then threw his head back and laughed before kissing her on both cheeks, the French way.

'Ah my petite amie. Toujours la même chose.'

And whispering in her left ear, he added conspiratorially, 'that perfume. I love it. Surely it must be called Forbidden Love.'

With a 'Felicitations', and a tight-lipped smile, Simone neatly side-stepped Hugh, reaching her hands out for Anne's.

'You are so organised Anne. This is a wonderful day. So many people here. And all this delicious food. How do you stay so calm? I must get some advice from you before Alan is 50; I'm worried it will all be too much for me.'

'Oh it's nothing, really it isn't. M&S are a godsend. Come on, let's leave the men to it and we'll go and find Luc. He seems less shy these days Simone. And so handsome in a quiet, unassuming kind of way.' Anne was keen to move out of the entrance hall and into the main sitting room.

A gong sounded. And again. And a third time.

Finlay ushered the kitchen dwellers through to the sitting room, switching off the lights on his way in, and placed a huge blue cake in the shape of a golf club on a silver tray with a monogrammed silver knife. Fifty candles flickered in the light cast from the very realistic looking 'log' fire. Anne used the remote control to start the DVD machine and the assembled guests cheered as the large TV screen showed a Marilyn Monroe look-alike singing 'Happy Birthday to you, Happy Birthday to you, Happy Birthday dear Hugh-oo, Happy Birthday to you.'

As Hugh blew with every last bit of breath, the guests made a circle, clapping and laughing, willing him to extinguish all 50 candles in one. Anne then fussed around cutting delicate slices of cake for the guests and organising Finlay and Luc to hand them out on blue china plates with white lacy napkins.

Hugh disappeared through the back of the kitchen

as if to the old servants' loo, and returned before the guests had drifted back to their various preferred corners.

'Before the older members head off into the advancing night, I'd like to show everyone how I plan to remain young at heart despite my advancing years.' And with that, he slipped off his unbuttoned pink shirt and presented his right shoulder to the crowd.

'Ta da!'

There was an audible intake of breath followed by an uncomfortable silence.

'Hugh. For goodness sake. What were you thinking about? How could you?' Anne's composed persona vanished in a trice.

And from his mother, 'What is it? A snake or something? It's hideous! You're not 21 you know. What will the Dean think?'

A Caduceus or Physician's staff tattoo covered the area of his tricep. A staff entwined with twin serpents, topped with a pair of wings. The symbol of the power to harm or to heal. Finlay punched the air with glee and then thumped his elder brother on the back.

'I didn't think you had it in you brother! The Main Man joins the 21st Century. Come on everyone, a big hand for The Healer!'

Noticeably loud and over-energetic whooping and whistling followed.

Anne's heels clicked furiously across the parquet floor in the entrance hall as she went to the cloakroom to collect the parents' coats.

On auto-pilot she performed the hostess duties. 'Thank you for coming, and safe home now. I'll phone you tomorrow Muriel. I'm not thinking straight at present. What on earth was in Hugh's mind? He'll have to get it removed. There's nothing else for it. How silly.'

With much muttering and shaking of heads, her parents and in-laws buttoned coats, turned up collars, pulled on leather gloves and braced themselves for the icy blast.

As she closed the front door, Anne took a few long, slow, deep breaths through her slim nostrils. Finlay caught her, steeling herself to rejoin her guests.

With a consoling arm around her shoulders he said 'You should know him by now Anne. He hates the idea of growing old and losing his looks. This is just a mini midlife crisis. It could be a lot worse.'

'It's just the shock of it, I suppose. I never imagined he'd do it even though he's always joked about having a tattoo. You know what he's like winding me up. It's just **not** befitting a senior consultant.'

'Don't worry. It'll be hidden at work. And with you at his side, he can't go far wrong. You do a great job. The perfect consultant's wife. Hugh would say that too – he often does. Anyway, cheer up. Here's something to put it into perspective.'

Luc, Alan, Simone and Hugh appeared just as Finlay tugged his shirt out from the waistband of his jeans, pulled it straight over his head and revealed a silver ring, with Japanese markings on it, pierced through his left nipple.

'That'll be an *ethnic custom* somewhere no doubt, but it looks damn painful to me,' said Hugh with emphasis, as the others stared in amazement. 'You might as well show Anne your tattoos while the shirt's off.'

Finlay's upper left arm was encircled by an intricate black design reminiscent of a wrought-iron arm shackle.

'And you should see the one on my left butt cheek! But I'll save that for another day.' Finlay laughed over his shoulder as he moved back into the kitchen, tucking his shirt into his soft denim jeans. Luc followed him, pulling a pad and pencil from the canvas bag over his right shoulder.

Alan poked Hugh in the chest. 'So – a tattoo is it, Hugh? That'll be something to attract the girls when you're jamming, I suppose. But you'd better not do too much of that (pointing to Hugh's gin and tonic) or soon you'll be needing some of the wee blue pills to perform!'

'As my trusted GP, you'll be the first to know Alan. But don't hold your breath. No problems on that score; ask Anne. Now – let's top up these glasses and get some music on. I can still boogie with the best of them.'

Alan and Simone moved away, shaking their heads in mock despair.

When it was time to go home, Simone found Luc in a corner sketching. He'd made several attempts to capture the intricacy of Finlay's tattoo, and was at the point of experimenting with adding it to the truncated arm of a classical image of the Greek God Hermes.

He quickly closed the sketch pad and turned up the volume on his MP3 player, risking his father's annoyance rather than engage in chat in the car on the way home.

Causes over-reaction to stimuli

Musselburgh. The day after the party

'Have you seen this Simone? Simone, would you just look at this for a minute? For God's sake, you can go back to sleep when I've gone. This is important.'

Alan slammed down the sketch pad on top of the patchwork comforter under which his sleepy wife was attempting to remain in a dormant state for a few more minutes. He knew she was a slow starter in the winter mornings, spending ages wrapped in her full length wool dressing gown, seeking warmth and comfort in several cups of black coffee, dark circles under her eyes. But today she'd better waken up sharpish.

Forced from her sleep, she reached out for the book with one hand, the other searching for her reading glasses on the bedside table, before she was able to open her eyes properly and sit up.

'Where did you get this? It's Luc's. He'll be so furious if he discovers you've taken it.'

'I went in to wake him up for school. The first call of many no doubt, lazy so and so that he is. And it was there on the floor by his bed. He must've fallen asleep sketching. But that's not the point. Have a flick through it. It's all nude male figures. What the hell's all that about? Is this from school or what?'

'Alain, Alain. Calm down, please. They're studying Greek mythology just now in his art class. These are all Greek Gods or Heroes.'

Simone flicked through the pages. 'Look, there's Jason, and Agamemnon, and that one's Odysseus. He's good you know. He has a real talent.'

Alan grabbed back the pad. 'Well, it's not natural to be concentrating solely on male nude figures. Don't try to tell me that it is.'

'Don't worry. That's just the topic for now. He'll be on to something new soon. And you know, nudes are very difficult to draw. It's a great discipline for an artist, Alain; it's called 'artistic anatomy'. Now put it back before he misses it, please. He's fine. A normal boy. Don't be so hard on him.'

Alan slowly exhaled. 'Ok. Maybe I was too quick to jump to conclusions. God, I need a break.' He ran his fingers through greying curly brown hair. 'Another week starts and another bottomless pit of work opens up. I'll be late again tonight. A pile of insurance reports. Can't put them off any longer, Isobel tells me. See you later then. I'll put this sketch pad back before he wakens up. I just hope you're right.'

As Alan kissed the top of her head, Simone was already sliding back under the bedcovers, glasses replaced on top of her stack of arty magazines. 'It really is nothing to worry about. And don't work too hard my darling.'

Mondays. No-one could have Monday off at the surgery. Too many patients *just have to see the doctor today.* The community nurses would have a list as long as your arm of issues from the weekend for Alan to deal with. Don't ask them to go out of their comfort zone, whatever you do. The receptionists would be squeezing in extras, avoiding eye contact in case you bawled them out. And Isobel, the long suffering Practice Manager, would be scurrying around with her furrowed brow and hunched shoulders, organising everyone *'for the benefit of patients. It's why we're here, in case you've forgotten.'*

And to think he had always wanted to be a doctor. Some sort of storybook hero, saving lives and making a difference. Now it was a good day if he didn't go home with a headache and reach for the whisky bottle. It was a great day if no-one complained about some aspect of the service. And it was a ruddy miracle if everything went to time and to plan and there were no cross words.

Even worse, it was the first Monday of the month. That could only mean a lunchtime practice meeting. It had to be on a Monday, the one day of the week when everyone was in the building, such was the appeal of hospital sessions and university attachments.

Life was simpler in the days when the powers-that-be hadn't heard of the *T* word. *Teams*. When the doctors decided and the staff just did as they were told. Now you had to involve the nurses and admin staff in everything. Get old retired Margaret in her blue blouse that was the staff uniform in the year dot to cover the phone for two hours while everyone ate the drug rep's lunch and balanced agendas and reports on their knees in the crowded staff room.

'The team' was getting bigger by the day. A new healthcare assistant, the Prescribing Advisor, the audit clerk, the community mental health nurse. Soon they'd be asking the cleaner – sorry, Hotel Services Assistant – to present a paper on 'cross infection control measures for the modern surgery.'

Mrs Smillie, a patient most inappropriately named, with her long list of ailments and her pained expression, had just left his room after taking up far longer than her allotted ten minute appointment slot, when Isobel Nicol put her head round the door and in that annoying nannyish voice reminded Alan that 'we'll be starting promptly at one, remember, Dr Fraser. There's a big agenda to get through.'

Thinking 'one of these days I'll throw the pile of notes at her mother hen face', Alan smiled wanly and assured her he'd be there.

The reps' lunches had become progressively less appealing since Tesco had opened in Mall Avenue. Their weekly offering, dumped in the kitchen in the familiar striped blue and white carrier bags, had become increasingly predictable. When once you might have had fresh cream meringues and éclairs from Beattie's, and filled fresh crusty rolls from the home bakery in Bridge Street, now they brought scotch eggs, cold and miserable-looking sausage rolls and mixed multi-packs of egg, cheese and ham sandwiches. If you were really lucky there were tubs of Rocky Road and Millionaire's Shortbread and 24 packets for the price of 12 Walkers' crisps. The reps from Pfizers, Smith Kline Beecham and the rest were going to have to start trying a bit harder if they wanted the partners to give them any time after the staff meeting. After all, it was only the promise of a free lunch that gave them any chance of doctor contact.

Alan grabbed a pile of patient records and a stack of prescriptions, checking on the way that his black signing pen was in his brown cord jacket pocket, the same jacket he'd worn for years. Who said men couldn't multi-task?

There were fourteen in the too-small staff room. The two young receptionists shared a chair, the Prescribing Advisor, keeping himself a bit separate, sat on the broad window sill. The health visitor was still out catching up on missed flu vaccinations. And one of the partners, Tom Windsor, was on the phone in reception. There was no point in waiting.

Alan took his seat in one of the four comfy chairs. Tom would have to find a spot where he could. The other full-time partners Helen King and George Dailly were busy signing their quota of prescriptions. And Susan, the part-time retainer, was flicking through The Doctor Magazine. Isobel had long ago learned that there was no point in sending out the agenda and expecting anyone to remember to bring it with them, especially the GPs. So she passed round a dozen or so copies, and moved the flip chart so that everyone could see it.

The team operated with a rotating chairperson. No-one had been willing to take on the job on a long term basis. It was Helen's turn today.

'Can we get started please? I don't know about anyone else but I've got a pile of work on my desk and could do without this today. So let's go through it as fast as possible shall we? Item one – staff refreshments – Isobel please.'

'Well, as you know, we've got a new cappuccino machine that one of the reps dropped off for us. So it means we can have proper coffee all day if we want it. But someone will have to take on the job of washing it each night so that we don't get food poisoning from the milk. Any volunteers?'

For once, all had something to say.

'No-one told *me* there was a coffee machine. When did *that* arrive?'

'I don't drink coffee.'

'Neither do I.'

'I leave earlier than the rest of you most nights.'

'Can't we ask the cleaner to do it?'

'It's not in her job description. And it's not a health board-issued item.'

'What about if everyone cleans the milk dispenser when they make their own cup of coffee?'

'I think we know that won't happen, don't we?'

And so it went on until Isobel sighed audibly and suggested, 'How about I draw up a rota then? Fairer that way maybe. And please try to stick to it. Or I'll end up doing it myself and I think you'll agree that I'm responsible for enough round here – and not just managerial stuff either. In fact it's a pity I can't give injections and prescribe drugs, then you could *all* go home early and leave *me* to see the patients.'

'Gaun yerself Isobel!'

'Ok, order, order.'

Jeez. Ten minutes on cleaning a bloody coffee machine.

The only saving grace was that he'd reached the bottom of his pile of scripts. Alan picked up the agenda for his first look at it.

Items two and three needed input from Mary the Health Visitor so were passed over for the meantime. Helen moved on to item four – proposed Directed Enhanced Service – a Minor Surgery clinic.

'As you may know, there is an opportunity for this practice to offer an enhanced service in Minor Surgery, starting from April of next year. We need to discuss the idea in principle today and then set aside some protected time to thrash out the detail of it if we decide to go ahead and apply.'

'Dr Dailly, your thoughts please.'

George unbuttoned his Harris Tweed jacket, picked up the three pens which fell out on the checked carpet, stretched out his long legs and leant back in his chair. 'Well. The way I see it, if I'm thinking straight that is. And goodness knows after a morning like I've had it'll be a wonder. But knowing what I do about general practice, and understanding the new payments structure, although that's a minefield in itself as far as I can see, there are a number of reasons why we should pass up on this idea.'

'And these are?' Helen had her eye on the clock.

'Well, you know we've had the premises checked over by the Primary Care Manager, and we struggle to satisfy the requirements for the recommended square footage in the waiting room. And in addition, when the cross infection control nurse was out last month she almost slapped a decommissioning notice on our steriliser. And then Kate here hasn't done her surgical update for the last couple of years because we've been too short staffed on the nursing side. And we're stuck for rooms at least every morning. So it seems a no-brainer to me.'

Helen, looking increasingly irritated, snapped 'I'm sorry George. Would you spit it out please!'

'Well what I mean is, how can we possibly offer a minor surgery clinic here without it costing us a fortune?'

'Alan – Dr Fraser – what's your take on this?'

Alan rubbed his right temple up and down several times then clasped his hands under his chin. 'I'll be brief and to the point. It's for all those very reasons that we have to go for it. There will be funds made available for updating equipment and premises. One-off payments to kick-start a new service, there always are. And then there's always training money available at the end of the year when the Board is making sure all the budgets are spent. We can apply for funding for Kate's course and for backfill. I already have surgery qualifications. In addition we'll earn more money through the DES payment scheme so that should keep you happy George, even if I end up doing the work. And if we don't go for this, those greedy bastards in the White Practice sure as hell will and we'll end up losing patients to them.'

'Isobel, will you check if Dr Windsor is free now so that we can get his view? Time's marching on.' Helen mentally checked off the remaining agenda items and figured that if she didn't keep the momentum going there would be the usual list of deferred topics passed on to the next meeting.

Isobel caught Jim Windsor putting on his Crombie overcoat and making for the exit.

'We're not finished yet, Dr Windsor. And we really need your input on the question of the proposed Minor Surgery Clinic.'

'Och, you know what I think about that Isobel. It's a damned disgrace that patients have to go from here to Little France for minor procedures. You can just talk on my behalf. I've got a sick patient to check on. You know how it is.' He winked and was off.

Isobel could read the minds and recite the familiar litanies of all the doctors.

'Dr Windsor is in favour of the new service. He thinks it satisfies the requirements of the Kerr Report for easier and more local access to patient services. However, he already works a full week and more and would find it difficult to take part in any rota regarding minor surgery.'

Helen ticked the item off her list and pointed her pen in Alan's direction. 'I think you can take this one forward Dr Fraser. We'll leave it with you to report back at the next meeting, okay? Now, the Christmas night out, and then the audit group report.'

The agendas were a joke. Or maybe the order of importance really did place coffee machines and nights out ahead of patient complaints and nursing reports.

Margaret knocked on the staff room door and entered with an apologetic smile.

'Dr Fraser, please. There's a request for a house call. It's the Clarks from Mansefield Avenue. Maisie could hardly speak.'

'Sorry folks. I *will* have to go to this one. Isobel, you can fill me in later.'

Margaret had looked out the notes for Jimmy Clark. He had terminal cancer and was on a syringe driver for pain relief.

'Thanks Margaret. Make my apologies to the rep would you please. I don't see myself being back before the 3.30 surgery.'

Alan Fraser – Dr Fraser to the staff. And in their view, grumpy. Too formal. Short attention span if it wasn't a clinical topic. Difficult to approach if you had a problem. And as for that eccentric French wife of his …well. You didn't know what to make of her.

But ask the patients? – The best GP of them all, according to the really sick ones. The malingerers got short shrift. And he wouldn't prescribe antibiotics for the common cold even if it was four o'clock on a Friday afternoon. And if you came in complaining about being tired all the time, he'd hand you an information sheet on *boosting your own well-being* and suggest you try it out for a fortnight before you came back to see him.

However, if you were Jimmy Clark and you were dying, he'd stop by on his way home, unannounced, to check on your progress. He'd comfort your wife with quiet wise words and listen to your old Mother talking about what a loveable wee boy you'd been before you'd gone to sea with the Merchant Navy.

You'd see the healer in Alan Fraser, the one who *could* make a difference. And you'd stick up for him at the local shopping arcade or in the pub when the others called him *offhand, patronising* or just plain *awkward.*

The insurance reports were still sitting on his desk, waiting to be completed, when Alan left for home that evening at 6.30. He'd been late back to the afternoon surgery after waiting with the Clark family for the undertaker. A surgery list full of minor complaints that Ethel the Pharmacist could have advised on if your Mother couldn't keep you right with good sound common sense. The National Sick Service it should be called. And sometimes the doctor was sicker than any of the patients. Sick at heart. And old before his time.

Chicken Chasseur with sauté potatoes and green beans didn't lift his spirits. Neither did three, or was it four, nips – or doubles more likely – of Glenfiddich.

Simone stroked his forehead later as she said, 'Don't worry my love. It happens to all men sometime. We can try tomorrow. You're just tired, that's all. It's nothing. Go to sleep now. Keep me warm. And all will be well. Trust me.'

May affect memory

The following summer

'One more bag and that's it, Hugh.'

'As long as you put the wine in, that's the main thing Anne.'

'Don't worry about that. Alan always packs more bottles than we can ever drink. You know he likes to take charge of that side of things. I've brought only my favourite Bordeaux – 2004 vintage – apparently last year was a very good year according to Jilly Goodsen. And just for your benefit I did put in a couple of bottles of Glenfiddich.'

'Ah well done. There's nothing to beat a dram or two of the old usquebae, after a day out in the cold Loch Tay drizzle. Are we ready to go then?'

Anne automatically turned round to check that the children were strapped into the rear seatbelts. Empty spaces now. Family holidays eschewed in favour of group bookings to Ibiza.

'Kenmore it is then,' she said with just a hint of a sigh. 'At least you won't need me to navigate.' Once out into the Kingdom of Fife, she began to unwind and drifted off into a light sleep.

'You were miles away Anne.'

'Gosh. I was in the Vendée. Do you remember that holiday with the Frasers?'

As they passed the Kinross services, she yawned and looked out of the window.

July 1992

Bright uninterrupted sunshine in the Vendée, the weather girl had said. Hard to believe it when the rain was coming down in stair-rods in Murrayfield Gardens. Emily and Andrew were already arguing as the Land Rover turned into Corstorphine Road bound for the bypass. Anne had the book of maps handy in the front seat pocket.

'Will you two shut up right now and turn on your Walkmans or get a book out! I'm not having this racket all the way to France.'

Behind his back and out of sight of the rearview mirror, Emily and Andrew mimed their father's 'yak, yak, yak.'

'And stop kicking the back of my seat. Before you ask, I can tell you now that the first stop will be at the services at Musselburgh to meet up with Uncle

Alan and his lot. And then we need to keep them always in view till we get to Dover. I'll need all my wits about me. So just pipe down and keep yourselves occupied.'

Keeping Alan and Simone's car in view was a challenge. If Hugh's Land Rover didn't do nought to 60 in eight seconds, Alan's Cavalier certainly could. And he kept determinedly ahead until Luc was crying with fear at the thought of wetting his pants.

'Please Papa. Please. Need to go pee-pee. Stop now Papa. Stop!'

'Aah, he's done very well, Alain,' said Simone, reaching into the back to stroke Luc's leg. Remember he's only three years old. There's lots of time, surely? Hugh's bound to stop somewhere too before long. Let's have a little break. I need some coffee.'

With an exasperated sigh, Alan pulled in to the services at Berwick.

A few seconds later, Hugh drove in smoothly behind him. 'After we leave here, let's just meet up at Blyth shall we? It's too tricky trying to drive in convoy. I'll wait there for you, Alan.'

'You mean I'll wait for *you!*'

Anne opened her eyes and stretched her legs out in front of her. Hugh turned off the motorway on to the A9, looking past his wife to check the left hand lane 'Okay. Kenmore here we come. That luxury lodge had better be five star. I'm expecting a jacuzzi, barbecue, water beds and satellite TV at the very least. What do you say Anne?'

'Simone booked it, but I'm sure it will be fine. It's a child-free development, so that'll please you.'

'Adults only pleasures then Anne my sweet. Got your accoutrements with you?'

'I'm not sure I had room for my neck massager if that is what you are referring to?'

'Just as well I packed the electric toothbrush then. '

'Or of course there's always the great outdoors beckoning. *I'm a lumberjack and I don't care, I'll shag my wife when I get her there.'*

'For goodness sake Hugh. Keep your eyes and your mind on the road please.'

'Come on Anne. The washing's all done, the place is spotless, you've cleaned out the fridge and disinfected the bins. No kids fighting in the back these days. Now it's time to lighten up and party a bit. I bet Simone's not half as well organised as you are.'

'Maybe not. But then Alan runs after her all the time, tidying up behind her it seems. He's still wondering how he was lucky enough to land such a beauty. And frightened she'll disappear off with one of those arty types she mixes with.'

'Ooh, ooh. Put those claws away. Let's just concentrate on having a good time.'

She smiled weakly. 'Sorry, that's not really like me to be so nasty. I'm sure it'll be fun. If nothing else we'll have some of Alan's legendary cooking. Maybe coq au vin.'

She drifted off again.

In the Vendée, Alan's coq au vin had been the start of it. And the five bottles of Chenin Blanc hadn't helped. It was a memorable night. The children had begged for and been gratefully fobbed off with burger and chips. Bed now! And they'd actually gone at the first telling, sleepy after a day at Le Plage de Boisvinet, running in and out of the waves, building and knocking down sand castles. Eating sand-speckled ice creams. Luc trailing behind the Scott children, as his short legs grew tired.

Anne had put on some Italian love songs and kicked off her white espadrilles. Simone, already barefoot, had freed her long dark hair from its large tortoiseshell comb and lain on the blue striped lounger on the terrace. Hugh had poured wine into the generous glasses as Alan, long chef's apron covering his knee length cotton shorts, checked the slow cooking chicken, the aroma of which had gradually filled the farmhouse kitchen and well beyond as it simmered away quietly over the whole day.

All was well. The world was at peace with itself. Time slowed to an alpha rhythm. Glasses clinked in toast to *family holiday! the sun! La France! old friends! le vin!* Eyes widened at the sight of the steaming casserole. *Bon appétit!* It turned into a very late and drunken evening.

'A touch of sunstroke, that's all.' Hugh grimaced as the morning sun came through the slats in the shutters. He searched the room for his watch and wallet, holding his head in pain as he found them under the rocking chair in the corner, beside his deck shoes, and under his shorts.

'Oh really Hugh? You look beyond awful. Surely it's more about the wine – and the Cointreau? Don't let's forget the Cointreau. Or maybe it was something you ate. Surely not the coq au vin?'

'Well you never know. You had wine too Anne. And Cointreau.'

'Yes, but I knew when to stop. Well, you're certainly not fit to drive. We'll just have to hope Alan is, or the children will be so disappointed. We've been promising them all week we'd take them to Château de Talmont Saint Hilaire. You'll have to stay here all on your own and miss the fun.'

Simone's reason – or maybe an excuse – was a migraine. No flashing lights but a dull heavy ache on the left side of her head and a feeling of nausea.

She knew them well, these headaches. Alan had often suggested Imigran. But she preferred not to daily medicate and relied on aspirin or Migraleve, a supply always in her various handbags.

Both Hugh and Simone remained in their respective bedrooms as the children sang their goodbyes and Anne and Alan loaded the Land Rover with picnic basket and folding chairs. The trip would take the best part of the day.

Around 1pm Simone wandered through to the kitchen, still holding her head, looking for something to nibble.

Sometime later, Hugh found her languishing in the shade in a hammock, ice pack on her left temple.

'Too much wine? Or just couldn't face another child-filled day of fun?'

'That's not fair Hugh. I really am unwell you know. These headaches come without warning and they take a day or two to lift.'

'Let me massage your temples and see if that might help. Move over on to the lounger but stay well out of the sun.'

Simone closed her eyes and made a conscious effort to relax, slowing down her breathing and focussing on her belly rising and falling in time with each breath.

'You're tense Simone. Let go. Just be in the moment. No worries, no cares.'

As her breathing settled and her shoulders gradually relaxed away from her ears, she became aware only of the sound of the birds and the distant beat of the waves on the nearby shoreline.

'Lie on your front now.'

Squeezing some sun tan cream into his palm, his hands moved to her shoulders, rhythmically smoothing and circling from her backbone up and out over her olive skinned shoulders.

'That's better. You're not so tight now. How does it feel?'

'The headache hasn't gone but the massage is very relaxing. And I just love to be out of doors. I so miss the sun.'

'Well, no rush to move. We have all afternoon and there's not a cloud in the sky.'

Hugh continued with the comforting stroking and circling, slipping her camisole straps over her shoulders and moving further down her smooth back.

'One of my colleagues swears by reflexology. I don't know much about it, but why I don't I try massaging your feet and hope that the effects travel all the way up to that pretty sore head of yours?'

'Oh, my feet are very ugly Hugh! I don't like anyone to touch them.'

'Don't be silly. It will be my pleasure.'

Simone turned over, sat up and coquettishly presented her left foot to Hugh perched on the end of the lounger.

He systematically rubbed each toe in turn, front and back, before using longer strokes on her slim foot and ankle. She squealed when he touched the sole, pulling back with a 'now, you're tickling me! Stop!'

But he simply put a finger to his lips, gently replaced her left foot and picked up her right one in both hands, as if it were a delicate butterfly.

As a warm breeze rustled lightly through the trees, their breathing became slow and synchronised.

Without a word spoken or a glance exchanged Simone lay back on the lounger. Hugh began to move his hands slowly up Simone's slim legs, keeping up a soft and regular pressure in long sweeping movements.

Time became irrelevant. The flowers, trees, birds and soothing breeze only a hazy backdrop. Hugh stepped out of his shorts. Simone slipped off her tiny white lace panties in one quick movement and the two cured their headaches and hangovers through an energetic quickie, their breathing growing more rapid and then settling again as they each reached a satisfying peak of excitement.

'It's been a very long time, my gypsy girl,' Hugh murmured, turning his face to look at Simone.

Without saying a word she rose and simply blew him a kiss as he still lay on his back, and with sandals in one hand, and panties in the other, passed through the kitchen door and made for the dark of her bedroom.

She slept well in the cotton sheets and awoke refreshed and headache free. Hugh could hear her, singing quietly in French, as she set the big oak table for supper.

2005 – Loch Tay

Simone had fussed around Luc before she and Alan left for their weekend away with Anne and Hugh at Loch Tay.

'Now there's plenty of food in the fridge. Some of my crème bruleé that you like so much for pudding. And pizzas in the freezer for when George comes round.' She wagged a finger at him and adopted a stern face, 'but remember – no parties. You promised. And I promised Papa.'

Alan had performed his customary check on the house, this time with Luc in tow and notebook in hand as he went through his daily routine one more time for Luc's benefit.

'Keep an eye on that gauge on the boiler. If the red line drops more than a couple of points below the black one, open that tap there and let some water in. And if it rains a lot – God forbid – check to see if that rone pipe is leaking and put a bucket under it. I must get up on the roof and clear out the gutters. At night before you go to bed, make sure all the TV and video plugs are removed from their sockets and all the lights switched off apart from that security one on the landing which is on a timer. Oh, and set the burglar alarm at night before you go up. You know how to do that so that you won't trigger it off getting up to the loo don't you?'

'Yeah, yeah. Chill out Dad. Nothing's gonna happen. Just go off with Mum and forget all about everything. I'll be fine. I'm sixteen don't forget and George'll be here to keep me company. He's a big lad who can fight off any intruders.' Luc lunged, twisted and parried his imaginary fencing partner. 'It's only three nights after all.'

'Okay. We'll go now. And remember …'

'I know. I've already been warned. No parties. I'll just make do with smoking dope and watching porny movies with George! Only joking, only joking! Now go.' Luc shooed his parents out of the door, waving happily as Alan started up the engine.

Alan scanned the rone pipes as he pulled out of the drive. They'd need cleaned and painted before long. That was the trouble with an old house. No end to the repairs. Just like The Forth Bridge.

'It's been a while since we went on holiday with Hugh and Anne. Four or five years maybe? Kenmore again. Same place although more of a chalet sort of arrangement if I remember. That was the time Finlay came along wasn't it? He was a godsend, taking the kids for all those activities. Left Hugh and me plenty of time for the golf. I can't remember what you and Anne did.'

'Oh we went shopping to that House of Bruar place. Anne was ecstatic – if you could ever say that about her – with all the cashmere. And reduced in the sale too. Then we went to the matinee one day at Pitlochry Theatre. A play set in France. Their accents were terrible. It was more like 'Allo 'Allo. But maybe no-one noticed.'

'And that was the year we had a cooking competition using local ingredients. I caught a huge salmon and grilled it on the barbecue. I can still taste it. Prize winning. What was your offering?'

'Crème bruleé if I remember. Yes ... raspberry crème bruleé.'

Simone had needed wild raspberries for her speciality crème bruleé. It was always better with the smaller, sweeter varieties found up in the hills than the ones from the Aberfeldy Co-op. The competition rule was that each cook sourced and prepared his or her own ingredients, using local suppliers or harvesting the environs.

Alan, having checked that there was sufficient charcoal for the barbecue and that the utensils had been properly cleaned, had been engrossed in a Le Carré novel. Anne had been at the nearby timeshare development having her hair done. Finlay had taken the children swimming at a freezing cold rock pool in Glen Lyon.

Simone had leaned over Hugh, reading a travel magazine in the reclining chair. 'Hugh? Are you busy? Would you mind coming with me to pick some wild raspberries? I think some of them might be out of my reach.'

A ploy? Or an opportunity. Had it mattered?

Simone had wheezed as she climbed up towards Black Rock, clutching the wicker basket in her right hand. 'Not so fast Hugh.'

'That will be the smoking Simone. Those horrible French cigarettes. You should give them up.'

'You should speak. I know you have a sly cigarette now and again. Mr Big Consultant you.'

'Maybe so. But only when I'm away. It wouldn't do to go into work smelling of smoke now would it? Anyway, I'm fit. Golf, squash. And the other – now and again if there's not an R in the month. You should take up something sporty. It would do you good.'

'You know I hate sports Hugh. French women don't do sports. Far too much sweating and looking untidy.'

'And what about the other? You can't say French women don't do that.'

'If you mean *making love,* well of course we do. Why do you think we have siesta?'

She had tossed her hair as she made to overtake him on the path. He had caught her sleeve and linked his arm through hers.

'Alan doesn't come home in the afternoons does he?'

'Of course not. Don't be silly Hugh. He works so hard you know. No time. No energy. Always stressed these days.'

'So no *making whoopee* for the Frasers?'

'Now you are putting the words into my mouth. We have our moments. But sadly perhaps not as often as we used to. That's life.'

'And how does that make you feel, gypsy girl?'

'Don't call me that, Hugh.' She had shrugged him off. 'We are fine, Alain and me. Don't you worry. Now let's find these lovely hidden raspberries.'

She had marched off, keeping ahead until the gradient increased.

'Simone?'

'Yes Hugh?'

'Is it true what they say about the French?'

'And what is that?'

'That a little frisson now and again is accepted as quite normal.'

'You mean, with another man?'

'Or woman if we're talking men here.'

'There is a place for it. We don't make a fuss. Everyone can benefit if the circumstances are right. But marriage is forever. That doesn't change.'

They had continued up the path between the fir trees, every now and then glimpsing the loch through the branches. Calm and clear today.

Just beyond the tree line, the path forked.

'Now which way, do you think?

'To the left is less defined. So maybe fewer people go that way and there'll be more rasps to pick.'

'Ok. Yes, let's go left.'

Simone had found a clump of low lying wild raspberry bushes just off to the left from the footpath some hundred yards from the fork. She'd begun to pick the berries.

'Here! Here they are Hugh. Lots and lots of them. Help me pick them.

'We'd better taste them first to make sure they aren't too bitter. Try this one.'

Hugh had popped a small ripe red berry into her mouth. She had savoured the taste, closing her eyes and touching her lips with her fingertips in a moment of apparent ecstasy.

'They are perfect, just perfect. Now you. You must

try one too.'

As she'd stood on tiptoes and leaned forward to put a larger berry into Hugh's open lips, he had encircled her waist with his arms and pulled her towards him.

'Framboise? Or frisson? You choose.'

The choice had been made the moment she'd dropped the raspberry and responded to his lingering kiss.

He'd led her to a sheltered spot a safe distance from the path and with the minimum of fuss, and having made sure the basket of raspberries was safely positioned, they had enjoyed the benefits of a sun blessed journey, on a soft grassy bed, from the slopes of a Scottish hill to the heights of the soaring eagle.

Then she'd skipped off ahead of him down the hill, basket swinging gently in her right hand. Apparently, still time to pick more raspberries for that delicious bruleé. Hugh had shaken his head and smiled.

May interact

Kenmore 2005

Anne slid out elegantly from the front seat of the car at the door of the Kenmore Highland Club Reception where an imprint of her M&S credit card was traded for two sets of keys. Meanwhile, Hugh parked the Range Rover Sport in one of the two designated bays outside the luxury lodge. The other one was currently unoccupied.

As she walked up to join him, Hugh said, 'I've texted the others to let them know we're here.'

'Are they far behind?'

'All Simone replied was "uncork a bottle of red. We'll be with you tout de suite".'

'Typical. I'd rather have a cup of Earl Grey actually. But let's unpack first.'

Hugh left his golf bag and shoes in the car, along with the tennis racquets. The booze he dumped in the utility room while Anne decanted the luxury hamper from Valvona and Crolla into the fridge. Observing with delight the smoked chicken paté, Orkney cheeses, feta-stuffed olives, Salar salmon and hand-made Scottish bannocks, he remarked 'We'll not go hungry, that's for sure. And with that huge plasma screen for watching the US Open, the golf course next door and The Old Locker Room with its award winning selection of Scottish beers at the end of the road, I know what Alan and I will be doing this weekend! Good choice Simone, wherever you are!'

Anne saw the Jacuzzi bath and the sauna cabinet through the half-open opaque glass door to the left of the utility area. Moving towards the nearer of the two large bedrooms, she was drawn in towards the outsize bed with its choice of pillows to suit all preferences and the pristine white cotton sheets. Dropping her handbag onto the bed, she massaged her brow, outlining her left eye socket and temple with her middle finger as if to wipe away tiredness and worries. A short while later, Alan trudged in, a case in each hand, behind a laughing Simone who immediately removed her pink leather pumps to luxuriate in the pure wool sheepskin rug which dominated the polished wooden floor in the lounge area.

'Now you can really relax Alain. Such a lovely room. And look at that view over the loch. So peaceful and calm.' She twirled around in her bare feet.

Alan gave the merest hint of a smile. 'Well, let's get this lot put away first eh? Is there a safe Hugh? Can't be too careful these days.'

There was a safe. And a double lock on the external door. Several smoke alarms all with functional batteries. A security light which floodlit the darker rear of the lodge. And a locking barrier across the drive for use overnight. Alan could rest easy.

Anne might just about identify Tiger Woods but certainly didn't know her Michael Campbells from her Sergio Garcias. Simone had one opinion of televised golf *ennuyeux à mourir* – deadly boring. There was a craft fair on in the local gallery where Simone suggested there might be some homemade scones on sale to go with a cup of Brodie's coffee, much more enticing than golf.

The two wives ambled down the winding estate road, commenting on the rhododendrons in their purple glory, and sharing snippets of their offsprings' latest achievements and escapades.

Emily Scott, twenty two, was on course for a 2.1 in Politics and International Relations. She was desperate to return to the Australia of her gap year to do any kind of work that would allow her to swim, surf, enjoy a *tinnie* or two and live mainly in shorts and bikinis.

During the summer break from his BA in Spanish

and French, her brother Andrew intended to take a crash course in Teaching English as a Foreign Language, thereby making himself 'a sure bet' for teaching jobs in South America or Africa.

And Luc?

'Oh, he's still my beautiful young boy. But not for long I fear. He wants to go to Italy to paint. He wants to tour the major art galleries of the world. He wants to see and experience the joys of life!' Simone's voice grew increasingly animated. 'I can only blame myself for encouraging him. But you know, he has a real talent for art. It's just a pity that his Father does not see it that way.' Simone threw up her hands as if in supplication to the heavens. 'We're working on him.'

Wandering among the Harris Tweed handbags, the Himalayan woollen hats and the Breton sweaters, Simone stopped to examine the paisley pattern shawls from a local weaver. She was particularly attracted to one of a rich cornflower blue.

'What do you think Anne? Does it suit me? Or would the green one be better?'

'I like the blue on you. You should buy it when you spot it. It might be gone by tomorrow.'

'Did you know, Anne, that the Paisley pattern can be traced back to ancient Babylon? The motif was a symbol based on the growing shoot of the date palm, regarded by the Babylonians as the Tree of Life.

Maybe it will bring some life back into my face which is beginning to lose its youth I fear. Yes, you're right. I will buy it.'

Anne turned her attention to a lavender-filled wheat bag.

They are natural and environmentally friendly. Wheat bags are highly recommended by doctors, chiropractors, osteopaths, physiotherapists and many medical professionals as a natural method of pain relief.

'Do you think Alan would recommend this for my sore neck, Simone?'

'You know what he's like, Anne.' She mimicked his deeper voice, 'Alternative therapy rubbish. Is there any evidence to support its use?' It was a pretty good impression. They giggled.

'Never mind Alain. Why not try it Anne? What harm can it do?'

The baking stall was near the back of the room. One of the local women, with high colour in her cheeks and a generous bosom graced with a no-nonsense pinny, was making pancakes to order. *All proceeds to the local Brownies,* some of whom were using their innocent enthusiasm and charm to tempt passers-by to 'please just try one. They really are scrumptious! We've had loads already!'

Anne and Simone ate one each from a paper plate. And then bought scones, a fruit gingerbread and a tray of Millionaire's Shortbread – Alan's favourite.

They walked back in companionable silence most of the way, Anne watching the spring in Simone's step. And Simone admiring Anne's impeccable neatness and classic features.

'Let's hope the golf is over for now,' said Simone. 'And that the British golfers played well, eh? Then everyone will be happy.'

Sadly there was no British golfer in the hunt. Alan's waning interest in the TV turned into a monologue of him tearing apart the new NHS Lothian, and Community Health Partnerships.

'Have you ever actually attended a CHP meeting, Hugh? In fact you just need to read the list of who's sent apologies. It's as long as your arm and you'd wonder why they should've been invited in the first place, and what they'd actually contribute if they were there. Do you know that if everyone turned up to our local CHP meeting there'd be over 30 people there? How can you run an effective decision-making meeting with that number in attendance?

'The doctors dominate of course. That's only right. So you get the midwife representative taking one look at the agenda and no doubt thinking, "sod that, I'm far too busy delivering babies to waste time discussing prescribing budgets" and so doesn't turn up. Or even worse if you've to sit and listen ad nauseam to the patients' representative warble on about some survey or other when he's got F-all knowledge of significance or bias.'

Alan's colour was rising exponentially the longer he spoke.

Hugh wasn't keen to get into the subject of work. 'Hey, hey. Give yourself a break Alan. Your blood pressure's going through the roof. We're trying to have a weekend away from all that. Have you no funny stories for a change?'

'Funny? Christ. You have *got* to be kidding? Have *you*?'

'Well, let me think. Did you hear the one about the clinician who had just finished a marathon sex session with one of his patients? He was resting afterwards and was feeling a bit guilty because he thought it wasn't really ethical to screw a patient. However, a little voice in his head said "Lots of other doctors have sex with their patients so it's not like you're the first..." This made the doctor feel a little bit better until still another voice in his head said, "... but they probably weren't veterinarians"!'

'Oh give me a dram. And make it a large one. That's dire Hugh.'

'I didn't think it was that bad, you old prude. Time you learned to lighten up a bit. All work and no play ...and all that. Any other holiday plans this year?'

'Well, nothing concrete. Two of the other partners have young children so they commandeer most of our so-called summer. Simone wants to go and see some sculpture exhibition in Paris so we'll probably have a couple of weeks in France in September.'

'What about Luc? You'll not be taking him with you I suppose if it's September.'

'Luc's going to be working on a community project somewhere in Glasgow in August. Finlay must have mentioned it. He was the one who put him in touch with the organisation. Disadvantaged kids I think. He'll be helping with the art side of it.'

'That sounds good. These kids of ours are pretty privileged. It does them good to get a taste of life on the other side of the tracks. I don't know what we're doing. I can't get Anne to commit to anything just now. She's always *too tired* to think about it. I think it's the menopause kicking in a bit early. I should send her along to one of my women's health colleagues. If nothing else it might improve her *appetite*.' He put the word in mimed parentheses.

Alan looked puzzled. 'That's not like Anne to be off her food. I don't think that's linked to the menopause.'

Hugh let out a big sigh. 'Not her appetite for *food*, you dickhead. It's the batting average that's reducing rapidly. Come to think of it, you must see a lot of that in your surgery.'

'Oh right. I get you now. Oh, don't start me on that subject. They all come to *me* in the practice. God knows why. Maybe because I'm not threatening in that respect, just a solid respectable family doctor who might not be getting a lot of it himself – *in their minds anyway.*' He was quick to add that codicil.

Hugh caught sight of Anne and Simone approaching the front door of the lodge. In an exaggerated whisper and with an air of conspiracy he cautioned Alan, 'Here's the girls back. Better park all that for tomorrow, eh? Plenty time on the golf course to continue – and the perfect setting – holes in one, a straight shaft, divots and balls!'

Alan was spluttering into his cut glass whisky tumbler when Simone asked quite innocently, 'Who'd like a little bit of something sweet with their coffee?'

The final day's transmission of the US Open didn't start until 2pm British Time. Anne decided to wander down to the old parish church for the 11 o'clock Sunday service. Simone fancied a leisurely Jacuzzi bath. The 'boys' could just about fit in nine holes at Kenmore Castle before a brunch at one.

While Simone was finding the jets of the swirling water rather more pleasurable than she had anticipated, the men were practising their strokes on the driving range before teeing off. After a few leisurely swings with his irons and woods, Alan made to move off towards the first tee. Hugh called him back.

'Hey, not so fast. I've hardly started my warm up. Wedges, middle irons, long irons, woods and *only then* some work on my short game. That's where you can best improve your scoring you know.'

'Bloody know-it-all. I'm more bothered about being finished in time for brunch. I thought this was a relaxing weekend. Of course I want to beat you, but not badly enough to miss out on my food. So come on. Let's go.'

Hugh made him wait until he'd practised a few putts before they made for the first tee. The course was considered one of the jewels in the golfing crown, the design benefitting from a landscape that was almost perfect for a golf course. The natural mounds with mature Scots pine, the mildly undulating fields, the location on the banks of the silvery Tay in beautiful Highland Perthshire, and on this particular Sunday, a clear blue sky with a very light westerly breeze.

After halving the first, they teed off at the second, hitting out of a mound of trees onto a banked fairway. Hugh strode ahead, his long legs eating up the two hundred and forty yards to meet his tee shot.

Alan was breathless as he caught up with him.

'Whoa! Are you on a mission or something? We're supposed to be on a nice day out, not a march against time.'

Hugh turned round. 'You're out of condition, old chap. Too much time sitting on your arse, churning out prescriptions or watching obscure French movies. You'd better watch out. Or your muscles will start to wither away. And we don't want that. Especially not your *driver* – or Simone might start teeing off on another course so to speak.'

'What do you mean by that? What are you getting at? Has she been saying something? Spit it out, why don't you?' Alan's angry reaction took Hugh quite by surprise.

'Hey, cool down, cool down. It's a joke, a joke. That's all. Look – if I was your doctor, I'd be more worried about your blood pressure. Have you checked it recently? I'm getting quite concerned about you. Seems to me that a lot of the time you're like a tinder box ready to burst into flame at the slightest scratch.'

Alan brushed off Hugh's friendly pat on the shoulder.

'You've always got all the answers, don't you? Well, my health is just fine thank you. And it would be perfect if I wasn't subject to a constant demand from malingering patients on one side, and a concerted attack on the other from that lot in the audit department, always trying to show the practice is not up to scratch. Bastards!

'Anyway, you can't be that bloody perfect yourself if your wife doesn't fancy you any more. *Too tired?*

In my book that translates into *don't want to.'*

'Oh really? I *don't* think so. I don't seem to have that problem elsewhere. The girls who come to the jazz festivals have their own nickname for me ...'

'I don't want to hear it. You're welcome to them. Now let's get on with this game, or we really will be late back. And that won't benefit either of us.'

With unspoken agreement the two focussed solely on the game, egos moderated in favour of friendship, each aware that they did not want to cross that invisible line.

Alan finished with one stroke to spare over Hugh. 'Good game, old chum. Time for a quick pint in the clubhouse before we head back.'

The patio table was laid with bright yellow crockery decorated with brown coloured hens, the coffee in the mugs was steaming hot and the croissants warmed enough to melt the butter without burning the mouth. Just as the men were taking their seats, chivvied along by Simone, Anne appeared armed with plates of Ayrshire bacon, leek and pork sausages, Stornoway black pudding, tattie scones and creamy scrambled eggs.

'Wow!' Hugh enthused, pulling out a chair. 'You've been busy, dearest. Just the thing to line the stomachs before we start on the beer. Now where's the tomato sauce bottle?' He winked at Alan and mouthed 'just wait for it.'

'Hugh, you know we don't put the sauce bottle on the table. If you must have tomato sauce, I'll put some in a dish for you,' Anne said crisply.

'Simone? Do you let Alan have the tomato sauce bottle on the table in your house?'

'No, Hugh. I cannot understand this Scottish thing. Tomato sauce? What is it? A mix of sugar and horrible colouring. I would never insult the chef by covering his food with it. Alain does most of the cooking in our house and it's so tasty I wouldn't think of putting this horrible stuff on it.'

'That's funny. I'm sure I've seen Alan put some Heinz ketchup on his burger and chips at the golf club.'

Alan kicked him under the table. Simone looked up from her plate. 'No. Never. He doesn't eat your fast food. So bad for the health. You must be mistaken.'

'So Alan does most of the cooking does he?' Hugh quizzed Simone as they washed and wiped much later after dinner.

'Yes. He enjoys it. It helps him wind down after he comes home from work. And I forget to eat sometimes, you know, when I'm busy working on a sculpture. I can spend hours in my studio, lost in my work, oblivious to everything else. He makes sure I don't die of starvation! He's a good man, Alain.'

She lowered her voice. 'Hugh? Can I ask you … do you notice that he is very stressed? I worry about him, and the effects on his health.'

'Well, he *is* on a short fuse. Flies off the handle very easily. I would try to persuade him to go and see his GP for a well man check. He certainly can't hold his drink so well these days. Look, that's him off to bed at ten o'clock. Not like the old Alan up late watching his French movies. No fun for Simone tonight, eh?'

'And none for you either it seems,' she retorted with a flick of the head. 'Anne is very tired. She's been saying the same thing all weekend. I bet she's asleep by now.'

'Oh drat. And I had the very thing to cure her tiredness. Now I'll just have to have a cigarette instead. Join me?'

They crept out of the kitchen door, closing it quietly behind them. Tiptoeing and giggling they ducked under the barrier and through a space in the rhododendrons, the sky still light in the west.

'Hugh, Hugh,' she whispered. 'Did you remember a lighter?'

'Of course I did. But you'll have to find it. It's in a pocket here somewhere!' He gestured towards his navy Craghopper trousers. With their eight pockets.

They made a game of it.

'Is this it? Oh non. It is your pen.'

'Is this it? Maybeeee. Let me feel it. Ah non. It is a golf tee.'

'Is this it then? Oh, I think that is something very different. Definitely not a cigarette lighter.'

'No, indeed. Something much bigger – and better.'

The orange glow in the sky had just disappeared by the time they crept back into the lodge. A solitary owl hooted. A dog barked in the distance. A jet bound for America flew way high overhead, its dozing occupants oblivious to the tiny figures far below.

A favourable outcome

2006 Edinburgh

Biography and Catalogue notes

Madame Simone Fournier has a grand passion for sculpture running through her veins. Her ancestors come from the Carmargue region of southern France, and she is half-Romany, a culture which, she says, strongly influences her work.

Raised in Montpelier, Simone was an artistically gifted child, forever drawing, painting and creating sculptures from whatever materials were to hand, which she would then give as presents or sell to tourists via a family friend's market stall. After leaving school, she dreamt of going to College to take a formal course in Art but didn't have the funds to do so. Instead, after a holiday to Brittany, she secured a post working as a hotel receptionist in Dinan, where she met one of the region's foremost sculptors in 1974, Antoine Rouault, who offered her the opportunity of a part-time apprenticeship in his studio on the famous Rue de Petit Fort.

Under his tutelage she was able to gain experience working with a range of materials, and discovered that she had a particular gift for figurative sculpture, despite no formal training in artistic anatomy.

Domiciled in Scotland since 1976 following her marriage to Dr Alan Fraser, Simone worked for ten years in Arbuthnot's of Edinburgh where she became the company's specialist in French bronze. During this period she also established her sculpture studio in the grounds of her home and become increasingly well-known for her exquisite bronze figurines, and, in complete contrast - her large outdoor wooden sculptures which symbolise philosophical concepts. Two of these, 'State of Nature' and 'Unity', were commissioned for Edinburgh's Botanical Gardens.

Simone holds a biennial exhibition in Edinburgh and has also exhibited in Paris, Dinan and Montpelier. She has been invited to London next year to exhibit in the Waterside Gallery.

The *Liberté* collection displayed here today within the gracious surroundings of La Galerie Européenne consists of figurines made during the last two years that have not previously been displayed. Simone explains the title: "I wanted to show how I believe women can find their own freedom. '*Liberté*' is an expression of how women search for their own liberty, which for many women is through self-indulgence, or by doing things they may never have thought they could do. For others, sadly, that liberty only comes in death."

Gypsy Girl - 2005 Black bronze, unique. 16" x 14"x 10": £ 10,000

La Feumeuse - 2005 Bronze, Edition of 5 (4 available). 10" x 10" x 5": £1,500

Cakefest - 2005 Silver bronze, unique. 8"x 5" x10": £2,000

The Flyer - 2005 Silver bronze, unique. 15"x8"x8": £5,000

Uncle - 2005 Bronze, unique. 10"x10.5"x 8". £2,500

L'amoureuse - 2005, Silver bronze, Edition of 10 (8 available). 8"x6"x4": £1,000

L'anniversaire - 2006, Bronze, unique. 10" x 10" x 7": £2,500

Third Age - 2006, Bronze, Edition of 5 (5 available). 8"x10"x6": £1,500

Serenity - 2006 Bronze, unique. 20" x 18" x 14": £10,000

Repose - 2006 Bronze, Edition of 5 (3 available). 10"x 6 x 8": £2,000

The Healer - 2006 Black bronze, Edition of 10 (8 available). 8"x 6"x5": £2,000

Dancer - 2006 Silver bronze, unique. 15"x12"x 8": £6,000

It's not Edinburgh's most prestigious gallery, nor its biggest, but it's perfect for her purposes. Chosen for its ambience and accessibility, and of course, the French connection – La Galerie Européenne – host to exhibitions by artists from all over Europe, keen to showcase new talent and those up and coming artists seeking mid-range prices for their work. Commission on sale only, provide your own drinks and nibbles (we will provide someone pretty to pour), booking fee £25 per event.

It's been a trying few days. Even with Luc helping it's taken so many hours to wrap up each figure safely and transport them (in two's) in the car to the gallery. Six trips in all, plus another for the drinks and nibbles. Now, for this opening night, all the pieces have been taken from the gallery's back room, where they were mounted on their plinths, and have been strategically positioned in the main gallery.

These figurines are her precious babies, each and every one. She alone has conceived them to a unique blue-print. She alone has fed and nurtured them, with her own hands, watched them grow under her loving eye, corrected them, enhanced and taken away from them when thought necessary. And she alone, after an arduous labour for each has given birth to a new being. They are made of bronze, but one would swear that if a first breath was taken then they would spring into movement, so full of life do these figures seem. That is the wonder of them, and it is that, more than anything, which has become Simone's trademark.

She is fiercely proud of her sculptures, and will defend their honour against any detractors. She does not bring anything remotely doubtful to exhibitions, nothing flawed, not even with the tiniest crack or dent. Every piece must be perfect. Those clay pieces that don't make the grade are discarded, left as poor orphans outside her studio, where they will grow green with mould and finish up broken into Alan's hard-core pile, ending up buried in one of his gardening projects. But the lucky babies, the perfect ones, fare much better. They are turned into bronze sculptures, and put on display for all to see; bought by wealthy clients, flaunted in 'magazine homes' where they will be admired and dusted and patted and passed on to future generations as heirlooms, for they will be worth far more once their creator is dead.

From the way Simone looks tonight, those collectors might have to wait eons for a return on their investment. She's polished, preened and dressed to kill, wearing a flowing embroidered lilac silk skirt, a low-cut (she must have a good three inches of cleavage showing) voile and lace blouse and a rose-pink military jacket with satin edging. A look topped off by her signature thick, dark hair that descends in luxurious waves over her shoulders and lapels. There is not another woman present who could carry off clothes like these at her age, and she knows it. She is everywhere, seemingly in all the corners of the gallery at once, talking and laughing, her hands moving animatedly in the air as she describes her work to interested attenders.

The young reporter is poised, pen and notebook at

the ready. He's been tailing her for about 20 minutes, trying to pick the right time to get her undivided attention and now he's caught her just as she emerges from the back room. 'Where do you get the inspiration for your sculptures, Madame Fournier? I can appreciate that they all come under the *Liberté* theme but they're all so different.'

'My inspiration?' Her eyebrows are raised, her lips pursed as if the question has taken her by surprise. It has not, of course – the answer, like her reaction to the question – is well-rehearsed. 'Oh that is easy to obtain, but perhaps a little difficult to explain, however, I will try.'

'I get it everywhere. I could, for example, be out walking on the beach – when I see a woman. She may be just walking herself, speaking to her children or her partner. Something about her triggers a thought in me. I might think ah – she is happy, or she is only pretending to be happy. She wants to be alone, or she would rather be with someone if she is already alone. And then I will get an idea for a sculpture and start drawing it out as soon as possible afterwards.

For example, from what we have here today, consider *La Feumeuse* – the smoker. I was strolling in the park and I saw a woman, maybe 25 years old, with three children. Two boys – aged I would think three and five perhaps, and also a baby girl who was asleep in her pram. The poor woman looked so tired – well – wouldn't we all if we had those three children to look after – but once the boys discovered the slide they ran over and climbed up the steps, then they went down the slide, whoosh, again and again, shouting loudly, whilst the mother has sat down on a bench and lit up a cigarette.

'As I get closer to her I see she is leaning back into the bench with her eyes shut, inhaling the smoke deeply and loving the calm it gives her. She is still tired, yes, but now she is in complete repose and so for half a minute she is free. She has her *Liberté,* until it is snatched away from her by the return of the noisy, demanding boys who will wake up the baby and the mother's work will begin all over again as she has to soothe its crying. But in the instant I have captured in my figure, that mother has *Liberté,* she is *Liberté!* So you see, even the most simple of circumstances in everyday life can be a source of inspiration for art.'

'Quite so,' the reporter says, smiling confidently, but wondering how the hell he will make sense of all that for his article. He'd best stick to something concrete for his next question. 'How long does it take you to make a figure?'

Simone shrugs. 'That is not such an easy question. It depends, you see. It depends on so many factors: the size of the figure, the complexity, whether I change my mind halfway through and have to back-track or even start again – it does happen. For example, this one here,' she strides purposefully across the room to *The Healer*. 'With this one I had no problems. I saw her in my mind's eye after reading about women healers through the ages and then I started work on the design. It all came together quickly – the face, the angle of her hands, and it is small – not life-size – but it loses nothing for being small – it is still a powerful work of art' (she emphasises powerful by raising her hands palms-up to head height and lowering them down with a flourish to shoulder level) 'so I was able to complete it in a month.'

'But this one . . .' She takes off at speed, heels click-clacking on the wooden floor, nipping sharply in and out of the people who are standing chatting and appraising the objects, with the reporter almost running behind, attempting to dodge them too, not always successfully, so he is left saying 'sorry, so sorry . . .'

'. . . this one,' she has stopped in front of *Serenity* and has to wait for the reporter to catch up. 'As I was saying – this one – oh it took a very long time – I would say a year, on and off. See the detail in the nun's wimple – all those folds, and all the individual beads in her rosary – and the chain – they are all to an exact scale – very correct. I wouldn't like to say how long I was making even this part. It was a labour of love. But I like her, this old nun in repose. So peaceful isn't she?'

Actually, he thinks the piece is morbid, but how could anyone possibly disagree with this sculptress woman when you can't get a word in edgeways?

'Yes, she certainly is.'

Simone feels a tap on her shoulder. It's the gallery owner, Belinda.

'Can I introduce you to some good clients of mine? Mr and Mrs Whiteman. They're keen to speak with you about *The Flyer*.'

'But of course.' She turns to the reporter. 'Excuse me please. I can answer more questions later and there is the photograph to be taken, don't forget – you *have* brought the photographer from the newspaper?'

'Yes, he's over there look.'

'Ah, good.' She smoothes her skirt down in an unconscious movement.

Belinda is growing impatient. 'Mr and Mrs Whiteman – Madame Simone Fournier. I'll leave you to chat now.' And then she is off to facilitate another introduction.

The man is short and stocky. His wife too. He holds out his hand and gives Simone's a hearty shake. 'Pleased to meet you Madame Fournier. You have some lovely pieces on show.'

She holds his gaze keenly. 'Thank you, Mr. Whiteman.'

'Johnny. Please call me Johnny.'

'And I'm Sheila.' The wife holds out a dumpy hand heavy with gold rings and bracelets.

These do not escape Simone's attention. She flashes her most charming smile back to Sheila, but only briefly; she knows it will be Johnny who'll decide whether or not to open his wallet, so she'll focus her full attention onto him from now on.

He speaks quickly. 'We're particularly taken with *The Flyer* and wondered if you had any connection with the circus – you've captured her so beautifully, I would have thought that you must have personally studied trapeze artistes or maybe even been one in the past?'

Simone laughs heartily, the sounds coming from deep within her throat. 'Oh there are no trapeze artistes in my family that I know about! But when I was a child my mother did take me to see the circus every year when it came to Marseille. Most children liked the animals best, but me – I liked to watch the jugglers and the trapeze artistes – they were so skilful and graceful. I've tried to capture that in the sculpture.'

'You've done that all right.' Johnny is smiling, he's already committed to buying the piece, Simone senses, as she looks him straight in the eye just that little bit longer than necessary.

'She's free as a bird,' Sheila chips in.

'Yes, that's the idea,' Simone replies, taking up the cue. 'She is so free up there – she has liberté in the air – so high – and with no safety net!'

'We must have her then,' Johnny states.

The first red dot in the catalogue. Always so pleasing.

'Belinda will see to it.' Simone shakes their hands graciously and extracts herself as quickly as possible without giving offence.

She has caught sight of Hugh and Anne entering the gallery and being greeted by Alain. She wants to welcome them personally into her domain, where she will be centre stage, and they – well, they will be upstaged – for once.

As usual Simone is effusive in her greeting, but tonight, in front of a ready-made audience, even more so. As always she is careful to greet Anne first. 'Hello Anne!' and a kiss on both cheeks. 'So good to see you – you look lovely.'

'And so do you. I just adore that jacket!' It's a genuine compliment.

'Hugh! Hello.' Again the double kiss, for which she has to stretch up on the tips of her heels whilst he leans over her.

'Bonsoir, Madame. Aren't you just the cat that's got the cream? Look at all these people. You must be thrilled so many have come. Let's hope they all buy! Now, where's the wine? Wine first, *and* cheese and biscuits I trust – I'm absolutely starving. Then I'll take a good look at your new babies.'

Babies? Anne gives him a puzzled glance. What on

earth is he on about?

'Hugh! You never change do you? You're incorrigible!' Simone laughs, shaking her head. 'It's always food first with you! The wine is over there – look – where Alain is already pouring one for you. Go on then both of you and I'll come and find you soon for a good chat.'

She wanders off to work the room, remembering that she hasn't seen Luc in the last hour. Where has he gone? He doesn't seem to be anywhere in the gallery, but there's no time to worry. Belinda is introducing another potential purchaser who is admiring *L'amoureuse* – a woman's outstretched left hand wearing an engagement ring. 'Yes,' Simone explains to the old lady, 'It could be seen as a paradox, but my intention with this piece is to show that for some women, marriage is an escape from poverty.'

Meanwhile Anne, glass in hand, has bumped into someone she knows from the tennis club and appears to be listening intently.

Hugh and Alan, standing in an empty corner, are deep in conversation bemoaning the latest NHS reforms which are affecting everyone. We Doctors are being forced to get involved in designing services, leaving even less time for patient care. Bloody government. It's all politicking. Haven't even had time to fully implement the last lot of reforms and now they're off again. Vote catching.

That's what it's all about. No rhyme or reason to it. Where's the evidence base that says this way is better than that? Hospital managers sucking up to Chief Execs, Chief Execs sucking up to the Scottish Exec. When will someone make a stand and say No – it can't be done in the timescale and not without more resources! What about all the GPs? Where do they stand? Some of them think it's a way to make more money of course, but at what price? Half of them are already almost burnt out. We're just giving away our power, or so it seems to me. So are we – I never used to have the trouble with the managers I get now.

It could go on all night, but Anne interrupts. 'Come on Hugh, time to look at Simone's wonderful creations. Alan – do you have a favourite?'

'I do, yes, but I'm not saying which. They're all good. She just gets better every year. I wish I could say the same for me.' He smiles benevolently but he looks tired. And he *is* tired, yet he's always the supportive husband, no matter what else is going on, so he's here, and he's dressed up, at least as much as he ever dresses up, and he will play his part tonight perfectly.

Hugh is casting his eye around the gallery. He dismisses half the figures from a distance then walks briskly over to *Cakefest* – a fat women with a treble chin who is holding a cake in each hand and chomping down eagerly on one of them. 'Ugh,' he says to Anne. 'That's ghastly isn't it? But good, nonetheless. It looks just like that fat cow behind the counter in the bakery on the high street.

'Hugh! Keep your voice down won't you?' Anne walks right away from him.

Suddenly, off to his right, he glimpses what he knew would be there. Simone has dropped little hints several times this past year about it. No wonder she was excited. It's utterly magnificent and he can't take his eyes off it. He leans over the figure and starts to run his fingers over her black, shiny head and down her long, smooth neck, but is brought up short by a voice whispering in his ear. 'Don't do that. You're not supposed to touch the exhibits.'

Turning he sees Simone smiling at him. In defence he whispers back, 'but she's crying out to be touched. Just look at her head, thrown back like that. She's clearly in ecstasy. And her body shimmering under her wet dress. Jesus, that is so sexy, Simone. And she bears more than a passing resemblance to you, *Gypsy Girl*, don't you think?'

'So some might say,' she responds, tossing her head as she turns away.

There's no doubt in his mind. He has to have this sculpture, and he doesn't care about the high price tag. It's surely been made for him, and he must buy it. She would have known he couldn't resist it. Crafty. Very crafty.

'Interesting, aren't they Hugh?' Anne has taken care to view all the figures closely.

'Yes. They are. And I've bought the best one, this *Gypsy Girl*. I'd better confess now. Stunning. It'll look magnificent on the new hallstand.'

'What? You've actually bought it? Hugh! We can't afford that much right now – we've just bought the flat for the twins and this is the most expensive piece in the exhibition! You should have consulted me first!'

'Think of it as an investment, darling. It'll only take a few more private patients after all to cover the cost, don't worry about it. It will set off the hallstand a treat. The cleaner will be horrified to see those nipples hey, not to mention your mother – can't wait to see her face next time she visits!' End of conversation. Then with a quick glance over his shoulder, he takes Anne's arm, and steers her away into the crowd.

'Hugh – I just wanted to say thanks for buying one of the sculptures. Simone is delighted. It's really made the exhibition a success selling the top exhibit on opening night.' Alan is saying goodbye at the door, as Hugh dons his coat ready to leave and follow after Anne who's already walked out into the street. Hugh slaps him on the back. 'My pleasure, old mate. You're a lucky bugger you know, she's some talented girl, your Simone.'

'Don't I know it,' Alan replies. 'Safe drive home. Catch up soon okay?'

They're both exhilarated after the success of the exhibition, and it's going to be hard to wind down. Simone throws herself on the sofa and kicks off her shoes. 'I'm exhausted, but in a good way! I deserve a drink now Alain.'

'Yes, you do and I'll get it for you – you just stay there and put your feet up.' He brings her a black coffee which he knows will not help her sleep but it'll be what she wants. It's the usual nightcap for him – a wee dram of Glenfiddich. He sinks onto the end of the sofa next to her feet, picks up one in his hand and starts to massage it methodically and gently.

'That's nice,' she exclaims, holding the other one up and wiggling her toes vigorously– 'and this one next please!'

Luc approaches the room, shouting, 'Do you know what's happened to the packet of crisps I left on the kitchen table?' He pops his head around the door and sees them cavorting. Forget the crisps. With an involuntary shiver and a shake of his head, he takes the stairs two at a time, not even bothering to say 'goodnight'.

Confident that he won't come back down now, there's no point in either of them doing anything other than shout goodnight back. Simone works hard to speak normally through her giggles as Alan shouts goodnight whilst moving a hand slowly up her leg to her knee, staring intently into her eyes all the while. 'Oh Alain, that's so good, those heels are a killer for legs,' she purrs. Adding in a whisper, 'my thigh needs a rub too.'

'That's best done upstairs then,' he replies in a low voice, 'where I can make a good job of it. You know how I like to do things properly.'

Simone jumps up and closes the lounge door then sits back down softly next to him. 'But of course, my good doctor. Let's just wait a while for Luc to go off to sleep. And while we do, we can amuse ourselves a little, perhaps, just like this,' she says, pulling his head to her.

Her tongue straight in his mouth was making him hard. How long before Luc went to sleep? He came up for air. 'Simone, take it easy uh? Half an hour's a long time to wait.'

'Nonsense. I know you've got – what's it called? – something power. I'm just warming you up.'

'Staying power. All right then, let's see how long we can go just kissing – no tongues though.'

'Spoiling sport you are. But I love you anyway.' By way of answer he wraps her in a tender bear hug then starts to kiss her neck and throat, working his way down the carefully arranged cleavage.

Less than five minutes later they are on their way upstairs, needy for the other's body, with thoughts of Luc conveniently forgotten.

With the bedroom door firmly closed they resurrect an almost-forgotten formula used in times of sexual urgency. He throws her on the bed and lifts her skirt up. He undoes his belt and takes his trousers and boxers off whilst she raises herself up on her elbows and watches. Deftly he pulls her pants down and climbs on top of her, kissing her face hard, almost bruising her lips whilst simultaneously rubbing himself against her belly and groin. She squirms around accommodatingly, kissing him back forcefully. With his erection established he moves slowly – in a little, out a little, until he senses she is wet enough to take all of him.

'Now let's see how much staying power you have,' she taunts.

'La Chunga, you gypsy you,' he gasps, a while later, letting his whole weight sink into her body.

'Yes, and I'm all yours, Alain,' she breathes huskily, before setting her lips around his earlobe and sucking on it as if she were a hungry baby on a nipple, at the same time pulling down on his buttocks to squeeze every last drop out of him.

Talking Therapy

Morningside, Edinburgh – later that year

Hugh checked his body from all angles in the full length changing room mirror. He smiled approvingly at his reflection. Oh yes, he could still cut it. Nearly 52 but no sign yet of a beer gut, age spots or a bald patch. The white tennis shirt enhanced his golden tan, the neatly fitting shorts his shapely legs and tight gluteals. His youthful appearance was getting harder to maintain but he now captured and mentally filed every bit of throwaway guidance from informal chats with colleagues in Trichology, Dietetics and Dermatology, fasted from alcohol every other week and behind closed doors used a male moisturiser. In fact two male moisturisers – one designed for the face and the other for the body.

Alan, on the other hand, and in a smaller mirror in the gents' toilet, scrutinised the bags under his eyes, the developing jowls and the slightly yellow tinge to his skin. Turning side on, he was forced to breathe in and employ a deep clench to his core muscles in order to fasten the waist button on his shorts. He'd have to wear his tee-shirt over his shorts if he wanted to breathe normally during the match. Given that it was some considerable time since he'd last played tennis, how he looked might prove to be the least of his worries.

They met up on court three at the Morningside club.

'I thought we might have to cancel given the recent rain. Typical Scottish summer,' moaned Alan.

'You're behind the times chum. It's Astroturf these days. Good drainage system. And it should suit you too. Easier to slide across court to meet my stinging backhands, and the play is slightly slower on these recreational courts. So you might just snatch a game or two from me. Not likely, mind you, given the state of that belly of yours.'

'Don't count your chickens. Looks can be deceptive. There's a reservoir of energy stored in there,' Alan replied, patting his midriff fondly. 'And a will of iron in these muscles,' he added, as he flexed his biceps. 'Your call – rough or smooth?'

Calling correctly, Hugh chose to serve first. Alan decided to save energy by sending Hugh to the far end of the court, using the time to loosen up his shoulders and move his head from side to side to free up his neck.

They began the warm up. After a few leisurely lobs, and some soft practice serves, Hugh began to tease his old friend.

'Take that. And that,' he laughed as he volleyed and smashed. 'You'll need to run a lot faster if you don't want to be slaughtered once the match starts.'

Alan wiped his brow, narrowed his eyes, clenched his teeth and prepared to battle.

Hugh's finesse was sometimes outclassed by Alan's sheer power. Alan's more ponderous runs often failed to connect with Hugh's baffling variety of serves. Maybe the time factor would decide.

Hugh won the first set easily, 6-4. All he had to do was to win his service games and break Alan once. Alan ran, skidded, reached wildly into thin air and only occasionally drew breath in a fast paced set where Hugh barely gave him time to settle into any kind of rhythm.

As they passed each other changing ends, Alan bowed in mock deference. 'Okay, well done. Beginner's luck though. I'm getting my second wind now so watch out.'

He took advantage of Hugh's divided attention during set two. A shapely, tall, blonde, young woman wearing a very short skirt was playing on the adjacent court. Hugh happily traded a few sloppy returns and a critical deuce point for the flash of her upper thigh every time she served or smashed.

Alan was all smiles at the end of set two. 'I knew it! I just needed time to get into the swing of it again. That's us quits now. Play you for supper?'

Hugh didn't let friendship interfere with winning. If nothing else, he had to even the score after the previous year's defeat on the golf course at Kenmore. The third set became a contest between Hugh's superior fitness and Alan's extra strength, with skill at the game playing a bit part.

Hugh kept his porky partner running; Alan put every ounce of power into his returns hoping to blast them straight past his opponent.

At break point in the 12th game, fitness won out. Hugh reached an impossible left hand passing shot and returned it well out of Alan's sprinting range.

Egos remained fairly intact. They were all square, if you counted last year.

'Here's a question for you Alan. Is there such a thing as the male menopause?'

Alan put down his knife and fork and finished chewing his mouthful of French fries. 'Well, Hugh, do you want my personal view, or my professional opinion as a respected long serving general practitioner?'

'Both – either. You choose.'

'Professionally speaking then. The jury is out. Men do not go through a well-defined period like the female menopause. They do experience a decline in the production of the male hormone testosterone with ageing, but this also occurs with some disease states such as diabetes. Along with the decline in testosterone, some men experience symptoms such as fatigue, weakness, depression, and sexual problems. Not too dissimilar to what women go through with the menopause. Hence the association. However, the relationship of these symptoms to the decreased testosterone levels is still controversial.'

'Good answer. You've passed your peer review, Dr Fraser. Congratulations! You can continue as a general practitioner for another ten years.'

Alan gave a wry smile. 'Oh wonderful. Why do you ask?'

'No specific reason. Just that it was mentioned in the Gynae consultants' staff room at work. A couple of the younger guys were ribbing us seniors. No women present so it was getting a bit bawdy. They were focussing on The Groper – that's Bill Grant – you'll have heard of him. He's on sick leave just now, reportedly suffering from depression. Hardly a laughing matter but the jokes were going round that with his flabby gut and thinning hair he can't charm the scrub staff any more, and if he gets in a nurse's knickers he can't keep it up. So basically, work is no fun for him these days. Now is that the male menopause or something else Doctor?'

'More likely that the younger males are much more attractive and sparky. He's getting too long in the tooth, old Bill – he must be our age now at least. He knows he can't compete and so when he does get a chance, his self-esteem or lack of it, is affecting his hard-on. All in the mind.' Alan couldn't resist a jibe then; 'you must be experiencing the same thing yourself old boy!'

'No way! I'm in great shape. I look after my body. Apparently the staff call me The Silver Darling.' Hugh coiffed his hair, tilted his chin up and turned to show his face in profile.

'I'm not sure *that's* a great compliment. The Silver Darling is a fish after all. Slippery and wet. Yuck. But then again, if the cap fits. Certainly not far from the truth.'

'Hey! Enough of that,' retorted Hugh, punching his friend in the left bicep. 'The *silver* is for my beautiful full head of hair and *darling* for how much I am loved. Although I have to concede that some of these younger guys are hot stuff, even to my strictly heterosexual eyes. Their wives are working so they can afford to buy flashy fast cars. They wear designer clothes, and keep in trim with the au pair. Tragically, my days as departmental dreamboat might be numbered.'

They each took a draft of beer while they contemplated getting older.

Hugh turned to Alan. 'What do they call *you* at that dead-end place you work?'

'You may well ask. It used to be Bonaparte – a play on words you know – the French connection and then bone for doctor. But I have a sneaking suspicion it might now be something along the lines of Grumpy Git. I haven't exactly been on good form these last couple of years. Maybe it's the male menopause after all. Well, let's blame it on that.'

'And what would the lovely Simone say? Has she noticed that you're turning into Victor Meldrew? And what about some of the other symptoms? A little less hard. A bit less often. Or maybe you can't even perform on occasion?' Hugh made the characteristic drooping sign with his right index finger, enjoying the juvenile banter.

'Hey. Who are you to point a finger? If I asked Anne, I bet she would say the same about you' and he made his finger droop even further than Hugh's. 'I bet it's all talk and no action with you too sometimes.'

Hugh leaned over as if to share a confidence. 'You mean, Simone *does* notice something? Honestly, Alan, you can tell me. Joking apart. If it helps to talk about it that is.'

'You know the adage. Common things commonly occur. So given that I'm stressed out half the time, you can expect that result now and again. No need to catastrophise at this stage. I need to watch it though.

She's a beautiful woman as you know. And a sensuous one. It would break me up if she looked elsewhere as a result of an occasional disappointment in that department.'

'She wouldn't do that,' Hugh assumed his reassuring bedside voice. 'I could bet my life on it.'

Fit for purpose

The Health Board, Edinburgh 2007

Kathy, the Organisational Development facilitator, rearranged the furniture in committee room 2 at the Board offices. The conference table seated sixteen comfortably although there were twenty chairs squeezed in. She removed seven and piled them in the far corner. The catering staff wheeled in the coffee and tea urns, leaving them next to the cups and saucers on the white-covered table adjacent to the front wall. There was a less than generous supply of fruit and plain biscuits to go with the refreshments; sausage rolls and Danish pastries sadly barred due to cost implications, thinly disguised as a healthy eating initiative. The flip chart, with a supply of marker pens, was prominently placed, and within view of all prospective participants, the word WELCOME writ large. She laid the meeting papers at each place. All set to go.

The new committee entered the somewhat featureless room in dribs and drabs, lay people first and clinicians predictably last. Only five minutes behind schedule, and with a positive smile on her face, and a purposeful energy in her voice, Kathy formally welcomed the twelve attendees to the inaugural meeting of the Regional NHS Research Ethics Committee.

She introduced herself before inviting each of the group to say a few words about him or herself, including something that might be surprising to hear. *It helps us get to know each other as real people.*

Hugh and Alan exchanged glances as if to say, 'Here we go again. The touchy-feely approach.'

With varying degrees of verbosity and self-importance, the group heard from Mrs Janet Matthews, (non-clinical scientist member and bird watcher), Dr Spencer Dailly (statistician member and Harley Davidson fanatic), Dr Wanda Fischer (psychology member and watercolour artist – beginner), Mr Grant McPherson (lay member and church deacon), Dr Barry O'Shea (secondary care clinician and hill walker), Dr Mitchell Cleary (secondary care clinician and computer gaming enthusiast), Mrs Margaret Kerr (nurse member and supporter of the Mercy Ships charity), Mr Scott Graham (pharmacist and amateur archaeologist), Miss Vera Mayfield (lay member and co-ordinator of a local writing group), Major Kenneth Brown (lay member and former high heid yin of the TA).

Alan, representing Primary Care, noticed a few strange looks when he mentioned French films as his passion. He was surprised at the persistence of such stereotyping particularly in this educated group. As a result, and ever the political animal, Hugh kept his interest in jazz to himself and cited the predictable golf as his hobby, before dropping in ever so casually, his position as editor of the Obs and Gynae Journal. Well? – he *had* been appointed the Chair of the Committee and would need to – what was the phrase? – *create followership*.

This meeting was proving little different to dozens he had attended over the years, particularly since so-called facilitators had been drafted in as God's gift to 'full participation, honest and equal sharing of views, suitable airing of all the perceived pros and cons, leading to a meaningful robust consensus'. Health Board rhetoric par excellence, Hugh thought. Where *did* they get it from?

The lay members soaked it all up. Hugh's mind wandered as Kathy, in a voice full of gravitas and suitable emphasis, quoted from the Board documentation the purpose of the committee: *in reviewing proposed studies, to protect the dignity, rights, safety and wellbeing of all actual or potential research participants.* She flicked over the flip chart to point to the quotation with its key terms underlined in red.

'Here's one I made earlier' whispered Hugh to Alan.

Easy to say but what do these terms actually mean in this context? Who would like to suggest what we might understand by 'dignity'.

Eventually – *was everyone was happy with that? Good* with an exaggerated ooo. They then clarified (if he had a pound for the number of times he'd heard *that* word over the years ...) the frequency of meetings, the numbers for a quorum (yes, yes – we know what a quorum is, Kathy), the role of the committee and the typical format of the meetings.

And before he knew it, Kathy was summing up and asking everyone for feedback on the meeting.

What – no actual business? Alan was bemused.

'How did your meeting go, my love?' Simone was lounging on the black leather sofa, feet tucked up under her body, flicking through Art Monthly.

'Phew.' Alan shook his head as he took off his Barbour jacket, replying over his shoulder as he went for a whisky glass, 'no wonder they want GPs to stay self-employed. We're such good value for money. That was two hours to do something that could have taken ten minutes. The Health Board for you. All protocols and procedures, and not very much action. Never mind. It's a session out of practice every four weeks or so. That means we can get a locum in to do my surgery and I can focus on something different for a change. It might even be quite interesting.'

And standing up to his full height, he put on his most learned voice. 'And *I* have an important role to play, when any research is planned which impacts on patients in general practice. Those academics can't just do what they like you know. *I'll* be there to tell them that straight.'

'Yes, you do that. One up for the GPs!'

Alan laughed. She didn't have a clue.

Pouring his customary three fingers of Glenmorangie, he remarked 'Hugh and I went for a quick drink after it. If nothing else we'll see a bit more of each other.'

From the depths of her magazine she murmured, 'that's nice for you both.'

'And how did your Ethics Committee meeting go?' Anne handed Hugh a pre-prandial gin and tonic.

'Fine, fine. The usual. It's certainly not the short straw anyway. We all have to take on some additional responsibility and this beats Public Participation or Finance and Performance Review. At least it keeps me up to date with what's happening with research in the area, and who's up to what. It'll come in useful one day soon when I'm putting forward some research proposal of my own that needs approval.'

'Mmm' Anne replied. 'Anyone I know on it?'

'Actually there is. Alan – Fraser that is. He's desperate to get out of practice and he thinks this might help him get an academic post eventually.'

'Really?'

'It might be enough but he qualified so long ago that he doesn't have his MRCGP and he hasn't taken a relevant Diploma in Public Health or Medical Education for example. He'd be up against younger GPs who have all of that and more.'

'Alan doesn't have his membership? I thought all GPs had to have that.'

'Not yet they don't. Although it's coming, you can count on it the way things are going, at least for new graduates. No, but it would be expected if a GP went for an academic attachment of any kind – in departments of General Practice that is. And that's where Alan would like to go, at least part-time. You know – he'd have a lot to offer and he's a bright guy. He really should have made it as a surgeon but he slipped up along the way, got up the nose of some consultant or other and must have had something on his record ever after. He didn't get the chance to go further than SHO.'

Anne raised her eyebrows. 'I didn't realise he was a frustrated surgeon. Poor old Alan.'

'And what about poor old husband? What's for supper? Or will we eat after?' Hugh winked and smiled at her as he advanced in her direction with arms open.

'Oh the food really will spoil if we leave it. Anyway, EastEnders is coming on. And you know how I *hate* to miss it. Purely for social commentary of course.' She neatly evaded him as she made for the kitchen, tugging at her skirt, as he watched the sway of her hips.

'There's no dessert by the way.'

'Oh I think there is. But we'll save it for later, will we?'

She shook her head, muttering to herself.

The Ethics Committee meetings settled into a functional format and a relatively efficient process over the coming weeks. Hugh chaired with his customary blend of knowledge and charm, coupled with a very slight air of benevolent condescension. He could rein in those who were liable to dominate the discussion with a 'let's just go round the table now for a single sentence each on where we stand on this one,' and if necessary would ensure that the meeting did not overrun by assigning specific discussion time to each item on the agenda. If he deemed it necessary, and to assert his authority in an almost imperceptible way, he would put on his silver rimmed glasses, lean into the table and spell out his point, frequently pointing his pen for emphasis.

Alan would rib him afterwards. 'Pompous git.'

'Watch and learn,' Hugh would reply, tapping the side of his nose with his right index finger. 'Watch and learn my man.'

Some six months later, Alan had cause to remember Hugh's words when the Vice Chair Janet Matthews took the hot seat.

'As you will have gathered from the papers already sent to you, Mr Scott has submitted a research proposal for ethical approval and as such is precluded from chairing, or indeed attending, this meeting.'

That was without doubt the shortest sentence she uttered throughout the two hour meeting. Why use one word if two or even twenty two would do my dear Janet?

Alan was tempted to slide some practice paperwork out of his briefcase under the table to make better use of the time. If only Vera, one of the lay members, had not been sitting on his left, sharing her thoughts with him at every opportunity.

'Oh, that project sounds interesting, don't you think Dr Fraser? Who'd have thought there might be a link between gum disease and heart disease?'

'Gosh, I didn't realise there were so many people in this area involved in medical research. Did you know that? Perhaps you did, being in the trade so to speak.'

'Fancy Edinburgh being the world leader in life sciences. That makes our job even more important than I thought.'

The committee approved six of the seven projects presented. The seventh proposed to investigate family history of miscarriage in the immigrant Asian population of the region.

Researchers intended to ask GPs to identify suitable subjects from their medical records. These women would then be invited for interview by the said researchers.

The committee's concerns centred on the ability of some of the patients to make a free choice about whether or not to participate in the research, given their poor language skills. They might be persuaded to participate by factors unrelated to the research itself rather than by any true assessment of the benefits or potential harm of participation. A desire to please the GP, a perception that if the letter came from the surgery then participation must be mandatory and so on.

Furthermore, given the possibility of some distress to patients associated with revisiting such experiences, there was no mention of appropriate counselling in their own language if necessary, to be made available if required.

The application would be returned with recommendations for modification before approval could be considered.

The meeting having over-run by half an hour, Alan was late joining Hugh at The Tickled Trout for a pint. His friend was already employing his best bedside manner with the Eastern European bar tender, a pale skinned, fair haired student of medicine in her own country.

'Give the man a pint of your best, will you Anna? And later you can pick his brains about being a GP in Scotland. Best job in the world, eh Alan?'

'Oh yes. Especially on the days when a locum is seeing your patients!'

The two made for the corner table, away from the speakers giving out some slightly out-of-tune rendition of the original out-of-tune 'Wonderwall'.

'Well?' asked Hugh, looking at Alan with a quizzical smile.

'Well what?' replied Alan.

'Well, did the Ethics committee approve my research proposal or not?'

'What about "nice to see you Alan. And how are things with you?" Or are you rushing out the door and haven't time to chat?'

'Sorry. I trust you're well, my old friend, on this lovely summer evening?'

'Yes, Hugh, I'm fine and no, you were knocked back this time, dear friend, Chairperson and esteemed top consultant. You'll get approval next time if you make the suggested amendments. Hugh's smile vanished in an instant. 'You *are* kidding? Aren't you?'

'Nope. You'll get the official letter soon I'd expect. Anyway, I don't suppose it's your own research project. You'll just have put your name to it to get the funding. That's how it works doesn't it? And of course the famous Hugh Scott will be first author on any papers you produce, regardless of who actually does the hard work.'

Hugh was momentarily speechless.

'No, that's not always how it works, Alan. I take a keen interest in my students and trainees. And I'm on hand to keep them right and give them encouragement where and when they need it. Nothing goes out with my name on it that I haven't given the once-over.

'So – which prat put the kybosh on it then? Or are you sworn to secrecy?'

'There were a few of us who had concerns if you must know. Older Asian women in this city often still don't speak good English. You might be seeing the daughters in your clinic when they have a miscarriage. They're born and bred here, talk with Edinburgh accents, maybe wear jeans and skimpy tops. But many of the older mothers still wear the shalwar kameez or sari and bring their husbands or children along to translate when they come to the surgery. So it was a fair point.'

As the light dawned in his mind, Hugh leaned in to make his point. 'And I suppose *you* were the one who gave the GP perspective, given that it's your territory? In fact *you* were probably the one who swayed the others, weren't you?'

'Christ Hugh. It's not the end of the world. Make the changes and it'll go through. No big deal, is it?'

'Actually, it is.' Hugh retorted. 'Put yourself in my position, Alan. I'm Chair of the Committee, and I fail to get approval for my own proposal! How bad does that look?'

Alan put his pint so hard down on the table some beer splashed out. He leaned forward and pointed a finger at Hugh. 'I'm going to tell you a home truth my friend. You know your trouble? Your ego is too big. You think the world revolves around you. We're protecting patients here, not enhancing research profiles or furthering careers.'

'What? That's bloody rich – from someone who's looking for any way out of dealing with patients. And if I remember rightly, it was your ego that got in the way when you fell out with old McPherson all those years ago. If you'd just grovelled like everyone else you'd have got that SR post and become a surgeon instead of a second-rate GP.'

Alan jumped to his feet. 'I don't need to take this. Fuck off Hugh. I'm going home.'

He grabbed his coat from the chair back, threw a

five pound note at Anna and made for the exit.

Hugh quickly caught up with Alan, where he found him standing in the lobby, fumbling for his keys, hands shaking.

'Alan. I was out of order. I'm sorry. It's been a hard day and I'm disappointed in the result, that's all.' He extended a hand. 'Friends?'

Ignoring the outstretched arm Alan walked away muttering, 'Maybe it's not that easy, Hugh.'

Recommended Guidelines

Later that year

Hugh emerged from the first floor stairway into a seething mass of suffering humanity. Damn. He shouldn't have stayed so long in the library. And he should have taken the long way back to his office via the car park. Now he'd have to plough his way – and worse, against the flow – through the hordes of patients making the tortuous journey along the out-patients main corridor to their afternoon clinic appointments.

It wasn't often that he saw patients like this; hundreds of them all together, with an equal number of different afflictions. Men, women and children of all ages. Obese ones, skinny ones, out-of-breath ones, ones with limps, geriatrics, some of them in wheelchairs being pushed by tired-looking carers, pregnant women, babies. Some patients were smartly dressed, others were turned out in dirty jeans and jackets and even dirtier trainers. But they were all headed the same way, with the same hope – to see a doctor who could offer a cure at best or at least some relief: a magic pill, or potion, a negative test result - anything would be better than what they were trying to cope with right now.

There were several members of staff negotiating the corridor who'd also got their timing wrong, and were now being given a salutatory reminder that despite the daily round of procedures, guidelines, protocols, codes of conduct, audits, planning and reviews, they were, in fact, really 'here for the benefit of patients'. He didn't focus on any of the patients individually, he just walked erectly, picking his way carefully through, wearing a generous smile on his face, and enjoying the wide berth some of them gave him courtesy of the white coat factor, which still worked for doctors these days, mostly if not always.

Then he saw her about twenty yards in front, walking towards him, that very pretty medical records clerk he couldn't help but notice in his own clinic last week. She was carrying a large plastic box heaped with files, and she looked stressed as she tried, unsuccessfully, to outpace the crowd.

Not far in front of her was a large family. A heavily pregnant mother, dad steering a pushchair with howling infant in situ, and three small, grubby-looking boys, pushing and shoving each other as boys tend to do; one second a tight group, then in the next, limbs flaying as their bodies ducked and dived around an invisible fulcrum. Their parents appeared intent on marching onwards, not noticing how their offspring behind them were upsetting the progress of other patients. Miraculously the boys still managed to achieve some forward motion in the middle of all this chaos, but their parents were now quite some way ahead.

Suddenly the smallest boy lagged behind and pushed one brother with all his strength full force in the back, then kicked his other brother in the leg. The resulting fracas caused an abrupt halt in the crowd, wrong-footing the medical records clerk who took a tumble, dropping her box and scattering the top layer of files all over the floor as the boys quickly legged it away after their disappearing parents.

Hugh arrived promptly on the scene like a knight on a white charger (in his own mind) to the rescue.

'Here, let me help you. Are you okay?'

'Yes, just a bit shocked, I think,' she replied.

He grabbed hold of her arm and deftly pulled her up onto her feet. Then quickly gathered the fallen files together.

Facing her, he put on his best reassuring voice. 'I've retrieved all the files for you; no damage done. Here, move to the side of the corridor and get your breath back.'

And before she had chance to consider his request,

he'd put his arm firmly around her shoulders and ushered her over to the window ledge.

'Right, take five here. They can wait a little bit longer for the files – at least you've a good excuse for being late with them now!'

She returned a wobbly smile. 'Thank you, Mr Scott. I'm fine now, honestly.'

'Are you sure? Carol isn't it?' he asked, clocking her name badge.

'Yes, quite sure. I'd better get going - I don't want to get into any more trouble.'

He'd have to give up on it for now. 'Well, at least the crowd's thinning out, but watch out for small boys as you go!' he laughed.

She smiled demurely, clasped the box firmly to her chest and without a backward glance set off once more into the fray.

Gorgeous, utterly gorgeous, he thought, but far too young really, or I'm too old, one of the two. Pity.

Any further reveries on the merits of young administrative staff were promptly interrupted by someone demanding his immediate attention. An authoritative women's voice rang out behind him.

'Mr Scott, isn't it? Can I have a quick word, please?'

He turned around to find a small, slim woman with sleek, brown shoulder-length hair dressed in a black trouser-suit. She was carrying a black leather briefcase in one hand, and the other was extended in his direction.

'Christine Adams. The Board's new Director of HR, as of last month. Pleased to meet you.' Spoken with an Ayrshire accent.

He shook her hand. 'Hello. Welcome to the club. HR . . .' He gave the name tag hanging around her neck a sneaky glance and read "Director of Human Resources". 'Ah – Yes, of course, the Hiring and Firing department.'

She returned a condescending look and with lips pursed, something akin to a cross between a smile and a grimace, her eyes flashed whilst she blew air out in a forced sigh.

'Humph! A popular misconception I'm afraid. That's actually only a small part – albeit an important one – of the widespread responsibilities of my *Directorate*, which is actually rather larger than a *Department*.'

'Ah well,' Hugh retorted, 'the reality is that what all you managers do all day is a little bit of a mystery to us clinicians.'

She jumped in, picking up skilfully on his lead and twisting it deftly.

'Well it shouldn't be a mystery. And I'm going to

make changing that state of affairs a very high priority in the next few months. You'll be seeing much more of me and my staff round and about this place. There are several important initiatives coming on-stream which will require effective collaborative working between clinicians and managers. We really do need to work much more closely together than has been the pattern in the past, for the benefit of both patients and staff.'

Typical management speak. He'd heard it all before of course. Same old stuff, but nothing ever comes of it. She did though, to her credit, look and sound genuinely enthusiastic; he imagined her to be a right little dynamo. At least that was different. But he really didn't see what this had to do with him and he'd lost so much time that afternoon already. Maybe if he asked her a focussed question about one of the initiatives he could then make a polite exit.

'And which of these *initiatives* will be of particular interest to the consultant body?'

'All of them! Without question. But primarily the design and resource allocation for the new wing, including the additional theatres – that should interest the surgeons. The outline planning and financial plan has been approved – so now we need to put the meat on the bones so to speak. Also there's the redesign of children's services – a big project involving the Council. I believe your

Department falls into that category?'

Hugh nodded.

'And another initiative that is HR-driven but will need to be adopted by all staff, such as yourself, who have managerial responsibility for others . . .'

He raised an eyebrow quizzically. 'Which is?'

'Could we just nip into the stairwell here while I briefly explain – it's a little more private than in the corridor?'

God, what on earth warrants this, he thought.

As soon as they'd negotiated the door and she'd seen no one was coming up the stairs, she said, 'A new bullying and harassment policy that will be implemented throughout every corner of the organisation and rigorously monitored to ensure it is being faithfully followed.'

Hugh raised his eyes to the ceiling. 'I can assure you that doesn't concern my Department – Ms? Mrs? Adams.'

'Call me Christine, please.'

'Christine. As I said, it doesn't concern me. None of that kind of behaviour goes on under my roof.'

She gave him another one of those patronising smiles.

'You could be surprised. The definition of harassment is wider than you might think. For example, I have to tell you that what I just witnessed between you and the clerk could technically constitute harassment.'

'What?' Hugh spluttered. 'All I did was help the poor girl to her feet after she took a tumble. How the hell could that constitute harassment?'

'Inappropriate bodily contact, I'm afraid, Mr. Scott. A tall, older male doctor, a consultant, putting his arm around the shoulders of a small, young member of admin staff. The new policy which we are adopting as part of the Scottish Executive's Guide to Good HR Practice in the NHS in Scotland clearly states that there is only one place where a member of staff can touch another that is deemed neutral in the workplace.'

He shook his head in disbelief. 'I'm sure you're going to tell me where that is,' he said.

'No, I'm going to show you,' she replied, extending her right arm, and raising it to touch, firmly with her palm, the back of his upper left arm. Their eyes locked. 'Here,' she said quietly, smiling broadly, more genuinely than before.

Hugh was quite taken aback. Actually, she looked quite attractive when she smiled properly

'Here's the spot.' She was still holding it. He looked down at his arm, noticed her slim, strong wrist and the stylish gold bracelet around it. Somehow, she seemed more feminine all of a sudden.

'Right,' he sighed. 'I'd best remember that in future just so I don't get locked up for inappropriate behaviour.'

She withdrew her hand. 'Mr Scott, now that we've . .'

'Hugh, please.'

'Hugh. Now that we've broken the ice there's a favour I'd like to ask of you. It won't take long, but your input would be extremely valuable both to myself and to the Board.'

He regained his composure. 'How long?'

'An hour maximum.'

'To do what?'

'To fine-tune the plan for the consultation meeting on the new wing with the consultant body. I understand from my staff that you've been here some while so you'll know how your consultant colleagues' minds work.

' I want to ensure this meeting is designed in such a way as to maximise their input and ideas and minimise the time they spend doing so, as I know just how busy you all are.'

When she'd asked so nicely, how could he refuse? 'My secretary Joan has my diary. She'll find you a slot.'

She beamed. Her unguarded smile really was quite lovely. 'Great! Thank you! Will my office be okay for us to meet? All the documents and drawings are to hand there. And we do a mean real coffee and chocolate fudge cake for visitors.'

'Fine. I'll find out where it is.'

'Thank you again, Hugh. Much obliged.'

She offered her hand once more and gave his a firm shake. Then she turned around and disappeared through the door back into the corridor, leaving him standing, slightly stunned, with the door closing slowly in her wake.

He blustered into the office, throwing his voice at his secretary as he walked past into his inner sanctum. 'Expect a call from the Director of HR's office for a meeting. One hour max plus travel time. Not this week. Too much to do and not enough time as it is. Oh – and a cup of coffee Joan would be super when you've a minute.'

He sat wearily at his desk and surveyed the large piles of correspondence needing his attention. He picked up his pen and went 'Eeny, Meeny, Miney, Moe, which one gets the Go, Go, Go?' But his heart wasn't in it so he simply shut his eyes, put his hands behind his head and leaned back into the chair.

Christine Adams. She was one sharp lady, no doubt of that. It wasn't often that any of the management people could keep his attention for more than five minutes, and on top of that, she'd basically bloody dismissed him, leaving him standing there feeling the whoosh of the door closing in his face. Half an hour ago he'd never heard of her; now he'd agreed to help her with a major initiative.

She'd played some subtle power game, he reflected. How had she twisted his arm without him realising? That harassment thing had been a bit strange. Then he remembered where her hand had touched his arm and realised he could feel it tingling.

Easy to Swallow

Two months later

By 1pm, and after three back-to-back meetings that had started at 8.30am *prompt* with the Senior Nurse Management Team, the air in Meeting Room 1 had turned sour. Words hung heavy in the air; reminders, promises, suggestions, threats. Worries articulated over deadlines, shifting goal-posts and staffing issues drifted around the room as invisible threads of dull energy, waiting to descend upon the next occupants who would feel instantly worse and never know why, the moment they sat down and waited for their meeting to start. The tea-trolley in the corner was littered with dirty teacups and saucers, crumb-strewn plates and a few plain biscuits past their best on the NHS standard white china plate.

Christine flung open the door with her free hand and rushed in, closely followed by her Personal Assistant, Moira, who was loaded up with papers in a rather large basket and hence in the absence of any free arms had to shove her foot in the door to stop it banging shut in her face.

'Typical. Just typical. Just as well we're early. Look at all this mess! Where's the lunch trolley I ordered? If that doesn't arrive in the next five minutes someone's head will roll! Moira – get on the phone to Catering will you and find out where the damn trolley is and tell them to hurry up!'

It was an order, not a question. The rising stress level of her boss had been noted. Moira put the basket down calmly and took a deep breath, strode over to the wall, picked up the handset and smiled before dialling, just as she'd learned to do in that Customer Care course last month.

One at a time Christine worked her way systematically along the length of the wall energetically thrusting open the windows and jamming the handles into the holders.

'How on earth can anybody be expected to work in this kind of atmosphere? Surely everybody's noticed the stale air in here? But nobody's done anything about it! Well I'm going to leave these windows open until somebody complains they're cold as someone's bound to. Better that than sitting here stifling.'

'I must give you a copy of that poem that's in the staff kitchen' said Moira. 'You know the one with the heavy black arrow pointing to the sink to remind everyone to wash their own dishes.'

This is a little story about four people named Everybody, Somebody, Anybody, and Nobody.

There was an important job to be done and Everybody was sure that Somebody would do it.

Anybody could have done it, but Nobody did it.

Eventually catering picked up their end. 'Oh Hello, this is Moira Armstrong in Meeting Room 1. I was just wondering if the trolley I booked last week for the Consultant's lunch is ready. Okay, yes, I'll hold.'

Somebody got angry about that because it was Everybody's job.

Everybody thought that Anybody could do it, but Nobody realized that Everybody wouldn't do it.

It ended up that Everybody blamed Somebody when Nobody did what Anybody could have done.

'Oh wonderful. Thanks a lot.'

She replaced the phone and turned around. 'Good news. It's on its way. They had a bit of a problem getting the cress for the egg and cress sandwiches apparently.'

Crisis over. The Director of HR pulled out her mirror and re-applied some red lipstick. A signal that she was, once again, ready for business.

'Right, put the papers out on the table, one for each seat. I don't know if they're all coming but I'm expecting ten at least. Remember to collect the spares in afterwards please, we don't want anything left hanging around and getting into the wrong hands.'

Then they began to arrive, the esteemed members of the Consultant body, mostly singly, mainly men, unless they had sent their Clinical Speciality Manager (usually female) along instead, and they came, almost all of them, exuding an air of hurriedness, as if they would really rather be somewhere else and this meeting was keeping them away from more pressing duties, such as dealing with the unrelenting flow of patients coming through their clinic doors.

On entering, a brief 'Hello' or nod was afforded Christine, then it was all eyes scanning the room for the lunch trolley, and greetings exchanged whilst grabbing a couple of sandwiches and a coffee / tea before finding somewhere to sit. For the tactically savvy this would be alongside, not opposite the 'Management', ie Christine, and, by now, also Alasdair Bain the Director of Planning; positioning which meant they would be able to disagree as much as they wanted into the centre of the table without having to face the two Directors.

Moira ticked off the arrivals she recognised on her attendance list and hoped she'd find out who the others were from Mr Bain given that Christine didn't know them all personally yet.

By the time Hugh arrived, and Christine was getting to her feet to open proceedings, the only free seat was right next to her, a situation he had already banked on, knowing how these things work, so he duly sat down with a casual 'Hello, sorry I'm late' and waved to a few people at the far end of the room.

Christine pushed her chair back loudly as a means of getting attention, stood up and beamed a winning smile at the assembled staff, making eye contact with as many as possible. Then she launched into a brief and carefully rehearsed introduction and short presentation before handing over to Alasdair.

'Welcome everybody, and thank you for coming to this very important meeting about the hospital's new wing. I'm well aware that we are all very busy and hard-working people so the intention is to keep you here for as little time as possible whilst gaining the maximum input from you about the draft plans that are on the table.

'For those of you that I haven't yet met, I'm Christine Adams, your Director of Human Resources. You will already know Alasdair Bain, Director of Planning; unfortunately, the other Lead Director on this initiative, Dr Robson, Medical Director, has had to give his apologies today as he's chairing a meeting for the Scottish Council in Glasgow.'

She pretended not to notice the muffled laughter at the far end of the table (due to a sotto voce comment that 'no prizes for guessing where he wants to jump ship to then') and moved swiftly across to the projector.

Slide 1, a futuristic building in silhouette in the background with the Board logo featured across the top stated:

Hospital Expansion: New Wing

The Scottish Executive has agreed funding for the project

The outline plan for the building has been drawn up by the architects

THE DETAIL IS UP TO YOU !

Christine drew herself up to full height and projected enthusiasm and drive into the room. 'We therefore have a brilliant opportunity to work on the *detailed* planning of services and accommodation to ensure that our hospital has a fit-for-purpose building of which our staff can be justly proud, and where all patients are able to receive the highest standards of care, in pleasant and well-equipped surroundings.

'Importantly, and I stress, this is not *just* about buildings. It's about examining the way services are currently delivered, and redesigning them to best advantage to meet gold standards of efficiency and effectiveness. And the Board is asking you, and all your colleagues who deliver our services to come up with the best redesign possible, because it believes that *you* are the ones who have the knowledge and the creativity to do just that. I'll hand over to Alasdair now to explain the supporting role of the Project Team in all this.'

Whilst she had been speaking, the room was silent. A few had scribbled notes, or potential questions, but in the main, eyes had focussed on Christine, not least of all the discerning pair belonging to Hugh. He felt she'd pitched it just right, that she had listened to his advice about the pre-amble and her delivery had been pitch-perfect, coming from that beautiful mouth of hers. Her habit of pushing the hair off her face and behind her ear when she was thinking hard made her look rather girlish and he found it utterly beguiling. As she sat down she glanced at him very briefly, surreptitiously, and he returned a smile; if he could have made a thumbs-up sign then he would have.

An hour later it was all over. It had gone pretty smoothly, all things considered, the two Directors and Hugh agreed. The only really sticky moment had been when old Ted Gibson had tried to wreck the meeting, stating that 'it was a complete waste of time all this token consultation because at the end of the day management would do what management has always done, ie ask people what they want and then ignore it.' Christine had gained Hugh's admiration (and no doubt several other die-hards like Gibson) for the way she'd handled the situation and been able to move the meeting on without alienating the old sceptic.

A consultation process for staff, with specialities tasked to collate and forward opinions had been designed and approved. There would be another, wider, meeting in three months' time to feedback the results of that and develop a broad consensus for the next steps in the design of the wing. Meanwhile, a patient survey would be conducted to ensure that guidelines for patient participation in the planning process had been followed.

Hugh had been proposed (a proposal he quickly accepted) as 'Liaison Clinician' with the Project Team, given his current role in overseeing the operating theatres, and since new theatres would be a key shared resource in the new building. And that suited him perfectly, guaranteeing him legitimate future access to Christine. For once, a member of Management with whom he wouldn't mind spending more of his precious time. The not-just-a-pretty face, sassy, sexy Christine, but the highly competent, ambitious Christine. And maybe, if he could get his own way, his Christine.

Fever

Leeds, 2008

He enters the dimly lit room through the side door and walks nonchalantly towards Lola. She is lying on the floor, naked, positioned on her side with her back towards him so that one bony hip is sticking up. She appears not to have noticed his arrival.

When he reaches her, he bends his long legs at the knees to lean over her and whispers 'Hi Baby, wake up, it's playtime.' With one hand under her left shoulder and the other clasped around her right hip, he pulls her upright – a little roughly – then in one deft movement, twirls her around to face him. With a practised eye he takes in every part of her body, appreciating her beauty, his excitement mounting with each passing second.

She remains perfectly still, makes no sound, as if she's resigned to her part in his game, but he knows that it's only a matter of time before he'll wring every drop of emotion from her.

Satisfied with the front view of Lola, he then twirls her round once more, so now her back is facing him. He runs the fingers of his left hand gently down her long, slender neck, keeping his other hand firmly on her shoulder. Now he's leaning over her, pressing his body into hers, sliding his head lower, over her smooth, brown chest, feeling all her contours slowly, sensuously, until he reaches her belly, where his hand pauses a moment, his fingers poised, ready to stroke, pull and caress until she throbs and cries out, over and over again.

His eyes are closed now; his face is taut with concentration as he starts to count out loud, so they both know exactly when it's going to start.

'A-one, a-two, a-one, two, three, four.' The spotlights flick on as Hef's fingers explode into action on Lola's strings, setting up the bass rhythm for the drums and piano to follow eight bars later.

Her wait is over. Lola is singing now in a deep, melodious voice that soars out into the crowd; her body and that of Hef's in perfect harmony with each other, they're really getting into the groove. Apart from his hands, with their remarkable dexterity, his fingers displaying a finesse of pressure, there is now nothing left of the surgeon. For the next hour at least, there will be no displays of arrogance, no assumed demeanour of gravitas, no furtive glances at his wristwatch when in conversation with other people, no concern for anything in fact, except for the music.

Had any of his surgical team been in the audience, they might have struggled to recognise the Hugh they knew; for in his place is a jazzer – stoked, sweaty and smiling, swinging away with the rest of the band and loving every minute of it.

As Take Five reaches the closing bars the audience bursts into applause. A hand appears behind Lola holding out a drink.

'A little something for you Hef – looks like you could use it.'

Hef grabs the beer gratefully and downs it in one. 'Thanks mate.'

He has one minute to light up and take a few quick drags while Billy the drummer introduces the band and the next number, and until the count-in begins again before they hit it with an upbeat version of 'Sunny' arranged by Hef himself.

Three more numbers and it's all over. Smokey Nights down instruments and leave the stage, but as far as the crowd's concerned that's short-changing them – they want more and they're going to clap and stomp until they get it. The band doesn't mind – they're high on the performance – so back they come and deliver not one but two encores.

By the interval, with their table already full of

empty glasses, the band is in self-congratulatory mood, for the promoter has asked them back again next year with a promise of being higher in the line-up. Hef rises from his chair, just a touch unsteady on his feet – as he takes the order for the next round. It's six-deep at the bar so he pulls himself to his full 6'3" height, in an attempt to catch the barman's eye and pushes into the throng.

'Hi!' a voice chips in from somewhere below his shoulder. 'Great set! You were really going for it up there with that bass of yours. Loved it!'

He looks down at her flushed face, taking in her badly cut too-black dyed hair and heavily-made up eyes, dangly earrings and a low-cut blouse exposing a fleshy cleavage. Estimates 50-ish, divorced, will have a flabby arse and is 'on the pull' – typical of so many others like her at festivals like these. Thinks, fat chance sunshine, you're hitting on the wrong guy here, but doesn't say it.

'Yeah, thanks, it was.'

He turns away. Where's that damn barman gone now?

She's persistent. 'Cool festival isn't it? Have you played here before? I wouldn't know for sure of course since it's my first time here.'

Maybe, but you've tried this before love. Surely you can come up with something better than that old chat-up line? He provides a functional answer. 'Yes, it's cool. No, not played here before.'

She's starting to annoy him. Ah – here's the barman – good. 'Two pints of John Smith's please, two pints of lager and two whiskies.'

'Single or double?'

He hesitates very briefly. Oh what the hell. 'One single, one d-'

She's grabbed him by his elbow now and is tugging it, like a small child trying to attract its parent's attention. 'Hey, sorry – I don't know your name – could you tag my order onto yours, please? I'll never get myself seen in here.'

Reluctantly he agrees.

'Oh – all right – what is it?'

'Two vodkas and tonic, one glass of white wine – large. Thanks a lot. I'll call my friends over – perhaps you and the band would like some company for a while and we owe you some drinks now as well.'

He forces a smile. He wouldn't actually, but maybe the others would. Billy's none too fussy these days, not since his wife left him for a younger model. By the time he reaches his table the friends have already materialised. Billy raises his eyebrows quizzically at Hef.

'The band has some admirers it seems boys,' Hef says. 'The ladies want to compliment us on the set.'

It's a tight squeeze, but somehow they're all accommodated into the group and introductions are shouted all round.

'I'm Lindsey,' the chat-up artiste says, 'and this is Louise' (also 50-ish, black-haired and flushed) 'and this is my baby sister Maddy.' Now that's more like it, Hef thinks, putting on his sweetest smile which he directs at Maddy like a laser beam. Blond, 40-ish, slim, wearing shiny, tight leather trousers. She's got nice teeth and big tits.

'This is Billy, this is Dave, this is John, and I'm Hef.'

'Assume you're all Scotch then by the sound of it?'

Billy takes on the role of spokesperson. 'Yeah, ten out of ten, Lindsey, except it's Scots, not Scotch!' He's already chosen. It's going to be so easy – in for the kill in half an hour he reckons.

Maddy sitting next to Hugh asks, 'Hef's not a Scottish name though? Is it even a real name? Where'd you get that from?'

Could he stand that voice? 'It's best you don't ask. It's just a pseudonym. I use my real name in my other life.'

'So what'd you do then' she raises her hands and makes quotation marks in the air, 'in this "other life"?'

She might look okay, but already he doesn't care for her voice, or her accent, or now, her line of interrogation. Better get it over with.

'I'm a doctor.'

'Oh yeah? What kind of a doctor?'

He sighs. 'A surgeon actually.'

'No kid! What sort of a surgeon?'

'Obs and gynae if you must know.'

Maddy shrills 'Hey – you two – this jazzer here says he's a surgeon – of women's bits! Ha ha – bet you he's lying!' No, he couldn't, even given her big tits.

'What? A gynaecologist?' Lindsey's face is almost purple now. 'You've got to be joking!'

'C'mon boys, back me up here?' Hef appeals to them in vain – they're sniggering into their pints. Only Billy lifts his head to speak and he's no help. 'You're on your own mate. You're the expert on women's bits, not us!'

Lindsey's really getting into her patter, her tongue loosened by the drink. 'If you're a gynae doctor then you'll have to prove it, won't he girls? Here's a question for you Hef – where's the G Spot? You should know the answer to that!' and then she collapses in a fit of giggles into her glass.

Raising his hand to his brow, Hugh pushes his hair back almost distractedly, then gives her a rakish grin. 'Oh yes, I have no problem with the answer to that question. If you want the medical explanation then we're talking about the Gräfenberg Spot, purported to be 1-3 inches up the front, remember that – the front, wall of the vagina. The research evidence is conflicting, but some say that when this spot is stimulated, it can lead to strong sexual arousal, powerful orgasms and female ejaculation.

'Alternatively,' he quickly lights another cigarette for good effect, before answering slowly and confidently, 'if you want the crude explanation – which I think you do – it's the spot up inside a women's fanny that if she's lucky enough to be fucked by a man who knows what he's doing then she'll have one big holy cow of an orgasm.' He looks around at the group, takes in the shocked expression of the women, smiles, then takes another drag at the cigarette before rising to his feet. 'And now, if you'll excuse me, I have a phone call to make. I'll catch you later guys, if you're still here.'

He's out of the building, down the street, round the corner, across the road and into the hotel. Not far, but enough distance for an escape. Alone in his room he makes a strong, black coffee by pouring two sachets into a cup of boiling water. The euphoria of the set has well and truly lifted. His head's pounding from the booze and smoke and he's irritated about what happened back there – for allowing himself to fall into doctor mode so easily when he's supposed to be doing jazz.

But she did set herself up for it trying to be so

bloody clever. Billy's welcome to her – G spot or no. He glances at his watch. Shit – 11.30 – she'll be anxious and waiting. Better phone right now. His hand reaches for the phone and he's dialling his home number as he lowers himself onto the bed, stretching his legs out.

'Edinburgh 337 1845'

He hopes he sounds sober enough. 'Anne – it's me. Sorry it's late – I got held up after the set.'

'Yes, it is rather late – I was just giving up on you and going to bed.'

Her voice has a tinge of frost, along with relief. He speaks softly. 'You knew I'd phone eventually. Don't I always? Hey – the set went brilliantly. Two encores! And the promoter was so pleased with us that he's booked us again for next year, promising a higher place on the bill.'

'Oh that's good then. Good for the band anyway. What time will you be back tomorrow? Just so I know whether to wait for you for dinner or not.'

'Hard to tell for certain. It depends on the traffic and who's driving – the one with the least hangover – probably me I expect – I've left them all still drinking in the bar.' (Brownie points for that, surely?).

'Well, shall we say dinner at 7? If you're not back by then I'll eat mine and leave yours in the fridge for later.'

'Great, thanks.'

'Oh – and did you remember to phone Emily this morning? To wish her Happy Birthday? She'd have been expecting you to call her.'

Oh God no. He rolls his eyes up to the ceiling. 'No- I – uh – completely forgot – the rehearsal over-ran and then we went straight for lunch.'

Silence at the other end of the phone.

'Look,' Hugh says quietly, 'I'll do it first thing in the morning, okay? You did send her a card didn't you? She won't mind. She knows I'm away at this festival.'

'Yes, I did send a card but no, I'm afraid the truth is that she will mind, even if she says she doesn't.'

'I'll make it up to her – get her a little something en route.'

'Right. Okay then. I'm glad you're fine and enjoying yourself. See you tomorrow evening. Have a safe journey home.'

'I will. Take Care. Goodnight.'

Click. She replaces her receiver before his.

Hugh takes a deep gulp of air then expels it slowly. Enjoying himself? He certainly was much earlier on, playing on stage; then he wasn't, once all those stupid women arrived, and he really didn't enjoy that conversation with Anne. What was that all about? He'd promised he'd phone before bed. And so he had. He'd been told off – twice. Predictably she'd asked what time he'd be back for dinner. He can't quite put his finger on it, but something was missing from their exchange. It's too late now – no doubt he'll find out soon enough if he's done something else wrong

He swings his legs over the side of the bed and springs up, then makes his way to the bathroom. Face check: hair, teeth – a quick brush needed here, a smile into the mirror. You'll do, Hef. One last drink in the hotel bar, see if there's any interesting company to be found there – he could do with some – this evening has all gone rather flat.

As he strides down the stairs, his mind focussed on finding pleasure, Anne's words have already leached from his consciousness, as has the thought that something was missing. Had he cared to consider it longer he might have realised that she didn't say 'Sleep tight,' as she usually did.

Good for you

Edinburgh, that same evening

Anne pushed the phone away angrily.

She picked up the photograph of her husband on his 50th birthday, champagne glass in hand and smiling to the camera.

Yes, she said. Good for the band. Good for you. But not much good for anyone else around here, you being so far away when I really need someone to speak to. And not just someone, but my HUSBAND. She stabbed at his face with her forefinger,

Do you remember what that means Hugh? Not just a pat on the head, or a peck on the cheek. Not just 'good old Anne' when you mention my name to your colleagues. And definitely not 'dearest' when you're speaking to me. Haven't you read the research? Husbands and wives who call each other 'dearest' or 'poppet' or 'little lambkin' tend to have slipped into a perfunctory type of relationship and don't confide any more in each other.

Oh silly me – I forgot – that little nugget won't be in the International Journal of Gynaecological Claptrap. I heard it on breakfast TV. You know, that programme we sad consultants' wives watch as our husbands go out of the door to live a real life, at WORK; having meaningful conversations with workmates, sharing jokes and stopping off for a few 'quick ones' on the way home after a day saving the female population from the dreaded clap or the fearsome prolapse.

She was in full swing now.

You should be here – now – with me. Your wife. You need to hear my news. You need to know that the little lump you discovered on one of your rare explorations of my small but perfectly formed breasts (once upon a time they were your little cupcakes, you said), that lump you thought would probably be just a small cyst, is actually CANCEROUS.

When you left for Leeds for that stupid jazz festival I went to see Mark Preston at the Western. You couldn't wait to get away. You weren't even listening when I said not to bother phoning when you got there as I had an APPOINTMENT. You didn't ask 'what appointment is that, dearest?' No, you just carried on packing, swithering over whether to take the black leather jacket or the brown. Nodding and yes, dearing at suitable points in the conversation.

Mark had seen her at the end of his regular outpatient clinic. He moved swiftly, arranging for a biopsy the very next day and rushing through the results so she wouldn't have to worry any longer than necessary.

I put on a good act, you know. You would have been proud of me – if you'd been there of course. I listened to the bad news, so sensitively given and with no pressure to respond in any specific way.

Mark had taken both her hands in his as he explained what the treatment might involve and how the statistics were getting better every year. And he had reassured her that an intelligent woman like she was would be able to understand the aetiology of the illness and contribute in all kinds of ways to her own recovery.

Her voice broke a little.

Intelligent, he said. And yet, you must think I'm stupid. You must think I can't guess what you get up to at these events. Hef, is it? Hef? What kind of name is that? And what kind of juvenile game do you think you're playing Hugh? Maybe you always wanted to be a musician. Is that it? Well, *I* gave up a promising career to be a doctor's wife, in case you don't remember. A – job – I – loved. That day you walked into the lab to check out if a rush job could be done on some very sick patient's blood, that day you looked as if the sky was about to collapse because it was a Sunday and you were on call and had only just started your first house officer job. That day you treated me like a gift from God when I showed you how the system worked and promised to put your patient's file on the top of the pile. And I was just a little bit in awe of this handsome young doctor. Or I would never have let you persuade me to give it all up to follow you on your road to the top.'

She looked around for a paper hankie. Sniffing she continued to address his image.

I was bright, you know. I had prospects. I could have become a forensic biochemist like Nadia. I was really interested in that. But I gave it all up for you. So that you could move from job to job in your scramble up the ladder, never having to worry about finding a new home, or schools for the children. You just picked up your briefcase and walked out of whichever door had Scott on the name plate, your mind already on your work and raring to go. Glasgow, Aberdeen, Edinburgh. Good old Anne made it all possible. So that one day you could go off to some tacky jazz festival and leave me at home all alone when I needed you most.

And any hope I might have had of picking up my career again, retraining or whatever's necessary, now that the kids have gone? Well, that's probably never going to happen now – IS IT?

Anne felt almost purged when she stopped crying.

Whew. Where did all that come from? I haven't

thought about my own career for years. I don't look back as a rule. I believe that you get up and face the day. You look forward. What's gone is gone. It's in the past. It's today that matters. And you've got responsibilities and things to do. People depend on you. That's your role in life. And I get well rewarded, of course.'

She lay down, her breath shuddering as the exhaustion hit her. Her body felt as if it were recovering from ten rounds in the ring. Aching all over. Her chest and arms in particular.

A good night's sleep would help. Although that was proving harder to achieve these days. Too hot or too cold. Restless legs. The false dawn after only a few glasses of red wine.

She reached over for her current bed-time reading – The Last Precinct by Patricia Cornwell.

A leaflet fell out. *For anyone affected by breast cancer.*

If you have a partner, you may find the roles within your relationship change. Some partners become overly protective while others may take on an almost parental role. They may feel they need to find out everything they can about your breast cancer, or remain positive at all times which does not allow you to discuss any negative thoughts or difficult issues. Others may cope by continuing with life as if nothing has happened.

I wonder how you'll be Hugh.

However your partner responds, it is important that you both try to talk about your concerns.

And use your real names – not dearest or poppet.

The next day Hugh was late home. He *had* warned her after all.

'Anne? Anne darling?' He dumped his brown leather holdall on the floor while he went back out to the BMW to retrieve his beloved Lola. 'She' was the only reason he'd bought the estate version.

'Anne? I'm back. And I'm starving. Any supper in the fridge? Sorry I'm late. The usual set of idiots on the motorway. We were at a standstill for over an hour. Some prat had a blow-out. Anne? Oh, there you are at last. How're things?

'Oh, same as usual.'

'What did you get up to while I was away?'

'Well, there was lunch with Norma yesterday. Then a game of tennis. Popped in to Mother's to check if she needed a lift to the supermarket. She was fine. Otherwise, nothing to report. How about you? Good trip?'

'Mmm. Let off a bit of steam. You know how it is. I was needing a break away from that place up the road. Much as I love the patients, it's a relief to treat women as people for a change and not walking diseases.'

'Meet anyone interesting in Leeds?'

'Not really. A couple of new bands that were quite good. And the usual suspects were there, all getting a bit older and greyer. Great to be home though. However far I travel, I always love coming home.' He rubbed his hands in front of the gas flame on the log fire. 'Be a dear and get me a whisky would you?'

He kicked off his brown loafers, relaxed back in his leather recliner and sniffed the peaty aroma before enjoying his first mouthful of the smooth single malt, as he waited for his pasta bake to microwave.

'Hugh?'

'Yes dear.'

'I was thinking. I might go away for a few days myself. Maybe next month. Not sure where yet. Just an idea at the moment.'

'Mmm. Yes.' He savoured another mouthful of the water of life, then spoke without looking up from his glass. 'Don't see why not. Who're you going with?'

'Well, no-one actually. I thought I'd try something different. A new hobby maybe. Perhaps one of these activity weekends. I could do with something to stimulate my mind a bit. I don't know – maybe chess or bridge. Or even philosophy. Don't you remember me telling you how I'd hated the idea that every student at Edinburgh had to take at least one course in a philosophy subject? I ranted and raved about how I was there to study science and how could philosophy possibly be of any help. And of course I ended up loving that year of Metaphysics. I haven't looked yet, but I've kept the Sunday papers so I'll see what there is on offer.'

'You do that dear. Now that the kids are away you should keep your brain active. It's all downhill once you reach my age you know!'

Anne left him to it, leafing through the mail, sipping whisky, humming the occasional jazz melody.

The following afternoon, driving rain and an easterly wind beckoning, Hugh fumbled with the catch on his briefcase as he put away the papers from the Clinical Leads' meeting at the Health Board offices. Most of the others were already out in the carpark, flinging their coats on the back seats of assorted Range Rovers and Audi TTs, ready to join the hordes on the bypass as they made for South Queensferry, Cramond or Haddington. Two or three cars had child seats in the back. The females' cars.

As he left the room, he felt a tap on the shoulder. He turned round quickly and found himself face-to-face with Mark Preston. 'Mark, good to see you. How's it going? Haven't seen you for ages. You must've been away. Surely not another lecture tour you skiving so-and-so?'

'Certainly not! How would Oncology manage without me with all these new targets to achieve? No, I just wanted to say Hugh that we're here for you too if you need to chat. So don't hesitate to give me a call and come over any day. I can see you in my office when my list is finished. Not easy for you I know.'

'What the hell are you going on about Mark? Think I can't chair this group or something? I've been on the Making Meetings Effective Course; you should know! I could write the book now myself after all these years. No, no. I'll be fine. If you can shut up young Wilson on occasion that might be a help, but otherwise I'm not losing any sleep over keeping this lot in check.'

'I didn't mean that Hugh. I'm talking about Anne. I'm so sorry Hugh. We'll do everything possible of course, and her chances are very good, as you'll know. But if you want to discuss it with me on your own, you know where I am.' And with a kindly smile, he headed off, leaving Hugh, for once, short of a smart quip.

'Thanks Mark. I appreciate that.'

Anne – Mark Preston – Oncology? His brain slowly made the connections. Phew. Now he got it. She *had* been strange that night on the phone after all. He'd better go straight home.

Unexpected side-effects

Two months later

It is exactly one week since he decided to do it. Now the time has almost arrived he's not quite as certain he can pull it all off. He won't have the help of a smoky nightclub or an alcohol-fuelled brain this time, and he realises it's harder to do with someone you know, rather than with a stranger you'll never see again, yet he can't hold out any longer, he must try.

He shuffles the papers on his desk, puts his hand out to the telephone to make a call, then pulls it back again as if the receiver is hot to the touch. Indecision isn't his normal modus operandi, neither is apprehension, but there's no denying the unsettled feeling in his stomach. He needs a cigarette, but can't have one until he's right off the grounds – these days even consultants are bound by the hospital's no smoking policy. He'll have to wait, but there's not long to go now. Five minutes and his secretary leaves. Thirty minutes and *her* secretary leaves. Forty-five minutes and *she* will leave. And he will leave in forty, giving him just enough time to be at the door of his car when she passes on the way to hers. It should be easy, and there's not likely to be many other people around at that time either.

It's 5pm on the dot. 'Goodnight Mr. Scott, see you in the morning.' Joan's voice sings out, followed by the sound of the office door closing. He exhales quickly, suddenly realising he has been holding his breath.

'Ridiculous, bloody stupid,' he mutters, pushing his fingers into his hair above his temples. 'It's no big deal.' But it is. He's spent a lot of hours thinking about this moment, thinking about her. There have been four meetings of the Redesign Project Team, and another two with just himself and Christine. He's been looking at her face across the boardroom table, across his office desk, and standing in front of audiences. Or catching her face in profile next to him in cramped meeting rooms. He's watched her red lips moving, listened to her compelling arguments. He's shared close whispers, passed and received their scribbled notes, felt knees touching. Over and over he's seen her turn people around with her act, and received the sexy wink afterwards when she thought no one was looking.

And he's watched her turn and walk out of rooms

in front of him. That luscious arse, in the tight skirt, or the fitted trousers – it doesn't matter which – either does it for him. Does for him. He *is* going to get inside them at all costs.

At 5.40pm Hugh unlocks his car, puts his briefcase in the boot, opens it and fiddles around with the contents, biding his time for a few minutes whilst he waits for Christine to arrive. He spots her turning the corner into the car park. She's walking briskly towards her car as if on a mission, in the way she always does, head slightly bowed, her body inclined a little, heels click-clacking purposefully.

He swallows hard, and hails her as she approaches, casually snapping his briefcase shut, followed by his boot lid.

'Fancy meeting you here. Long-time no see! How's my favourite Director today?'

She halts, smiles, but does not put her briefcase down. 'I'm fine, thank you Hugh, but your memory must be failing – I saw you yesterday remember? The RPT meeting – surely you haven't forgotten already, given that you have several action points against your name?'

He taps his hand against his temple in mock surprise at his 'lack of recall'. 'Ah. . Yes . . but of course, so I do. Although . .' he pauses for effect – 'the meeting is hazy, my dear Christine, but on the other hand, you . . .' and projects his best, sexiest smile, 'Are always on my mind.'

She deflects his gaze by looking down as she adjusts the shoulder strap on her handbag.

'I must get on Hugh. I've lots of things to do tonight, including some papers to read through for the morning's SMT meeting. See you.'

She attempts to walk past him but he's too fast for her. He steps into her path and stands firm, still smiling, although after this rebuff it's taking more of an effort to keep his smiley face fixed.

'Hey, not so fast my pretty one! I'm sure they can wait a while. How about we go for a little drink someplace and relax a bit, forget about work just for an hour? I could do with some intelligent company after the day I've just had!'

She returns his smile with a stern look and draws herself up to her full height. 'Sorry Hugh. No deal. You don't seem to be getting it. Work is work. Home is home. I don't mix them, and I don't encourage colleagues to do so either. Afraid you'll have to count me out.'

He doesn't move, other than to put out his arm and grab her briefcase handle from her with a quick movement of his hand.

'Come on Christine. I thought we knew each other better than this by now – you don't have to pull the straight-laced Director stuff with me. We're friends, remember? We've done a lot of work together recently. We like each other; we're on the same wavelength. All I'm asking is that you spend a little time with me outside this damn hospital. If not tonight, then name your time – and place. I've had the impression for a little while now that you'd like to do that – right? There's no harm in asking!'

'Take your hand off my case Hugh.' She speaks softly, but firmly. 'We're colleagues, plain and simple. Any different impression you may hold is purely in your own imagination and has NOT been given by me. Now please . . . before you say anything more you may regret later, move out of my way and let me get to my car.'

His mind races – how should he play this now? He tries again. 'Of course, Sweetie, but let me carry your case for you. Don't make such a fuss, it doesn't become you.' He seems unaware that he's got it completely wrong.

She looks around the carpark, almost empty, and growing darker by the minute. She breathes out slowly.

'Right. Okay. Fine.' She releases her grip on the handle and marches over to her car, clicking the key a few yards out, and then opens one of the back doors as soon as she reaches it.

'Put it on the back seat for me would you? Thanks. Goodnight Hugh. I'm going home now, it's getting rather late.'

He grabs her shoulder so forcefully that she's

caught a little off-balance and almost bounces her head off his chest as he turns her to face him. She pulls hard to extricate herself from his grip.

'Christine.' He maintains his hold. His voice is soft and low, uncharacteristically pleading. 'Why are you being like this? How long do you expect me to carry on waiting? You've been flirting with me ever since I first met you in the corridor that day. You know you have. One of us has to make a move. That's all I'm doing, taking the initiative here.'

She looks up at him coldly, her eyes set hard, lips pursed. 'No Hugh. That's a lie. I've given you no encouragement of the sort, and I can tell you right here and now that your attention is unwelcome and unwanted. You are a work colleague to me, that's all, albeit a valued one. On behalf of the organisation, I'm grateful for all that you've done to assist with the Redesign. But that thank you is a formal one.'

She's still glaring at him.

Underneath his hand he feels her body tense even more as she takes a deep breath before continuing. 'There will not, and will never be, any informal or illicit 'thank yous'. I warned you ages ago that NHS Lothian's Bullying and Harassment Policy states there is only ONE neutral place where a member of staff can touch another and right now your hand is NOT on it. Best you remove it I think.'

His brain whirrs. Her shoulder feels so taut it

could explode and break his hand into a million tiny pieces. He lifts his hand off and steps back a pace, finally realising that he's made a grave error of judgement. He looks at her carefully and sees not her usual sweetness, or sexiness, but instead a hard, stony face with the shutters firmly down. And then it dawns on him – she's been playing him along – all this time. Sneaky bitch. Using clever management tactics, and feminine wiles to best advantage. What a fool he's been. He flushes with anger, feels his blood pressure rising.

'Ah – I see it now. Oh Yes, Ms Director of Human Resources, Ms Christine bloody Adams. I get what you've been playing at all these weeks. And I have to tell you I am not a happy chappie to be feeling like this – which is more than a little used.' He waves his arm outwards and bows low towards her in an extravagant gesture. 'On you go then. Just don't ask me to do anything for you again.' He slams her car door, throws in a louder 'Ever!' and turns on his heel to walk swiftly to his own.

She bundles herself quickly into the driving seat and locks her doors, pausing only to watch him speed off out of the car park, tyres screeching.

As she puts on her seat belt her hands are trembling. She takes a few slow deep breaths and then rifles through her handbag to find her small moleskin notebook and blue Parker pen.

She frames up a format for her notes.

What happened?

What sense do you make of it?

What have you learned?

What might you do differently next time?

'Isn't it a bit early for the hard stuff, Hugh?'

He pauses mid-pour of the whisky bottle, but doesn't turn around. In his mind's eye he can see his wife's pale face, her lips tight in disapproval. She's probably standing with her arms folded as well.

'Hello to you too Anne,' he replies tersely, 'and no it's not bit early, not after the day I've had.'

She shuts her eyes, shakes her head and turns to walk away leaving him drinking while she returns to the kitchen to finish preparing their dinner.

Hugh slumps into the armchair, glass in hand, takes a deep breath, then raises the glass to his lips and drains it dry.

'So,' he murmurs, 'it's come to this.'

For the first time in his life that he can remember, he's experienced female rejection (other than Anne's usual pleas of being too tired, having a headache and the thousand other excuses he's come to expect these days, given her illness). He must be losing it. He has no idea what Christine will do next – it could be anything, or nothing. Hopefully the latter – he really doesn't want any more hassle in his life right now. The one thing of which he is absolutely certain is that this is the last time he will play ball with the management. They'd have to go on their knees and beg him next time they want his support, then he'd take the greatest satisfaction in smiling sweetly and telling them 'No, sorry, that isn't going to be possible, not possible at all.'

Comorbidity

The Western General Hospital, late 2009

Picking up the remote from her bedside locker, Anne flicked from channel to channel, her eyes on the small TV screen suspended from the ceiling above her hospital bed.

Gladys in the adjacent bed leant over in her direction.

'Daytime TV? It's woeful isn't it – even when you've no energy to do anything else?'

'I should know,' laughed Anne 'after twelve weeks of it, but I keep hoping!'

She pressed the Off button.

'Visiting time soon,' she yawned 'and then it will be more of *Does the time pass quickly?*

'How do you find the food in here?

'I thought you might like some grapes? Or maybe you're not allowed these?

'How are we today Mrs Scott? Had a better night did we?'

'I know what you mean,' sympathised Gladys. 'It's all so meaningless. All I want to do is rest. And I'm really not interested in any of their time-filling trivia.'

'They'd have to walk a mile in our shoes to have any idea what it's like.'

'You certainly have lots of visitors Anne.'

'Oh yes, there's Hilary. And Caroline. Oh and Helena. And even Simone. Taking a few minutes out of their busy lives to just pop in and *see how we are darling*. You'll have heard them.

'Oh Anne. I tell you. If only I had more time. There are jobs I'll simply never get round to doing. You know darling, life is such a whirl these days. I just don't know how I can fit it all in.

'I feel like saying to them "You know what girls? – try being ill. Try having your body totally zapped by a noxious cocktail of drugs.

"Try almost dying from the treatment so as possibly to rise *(well there are no guarantees but we're hopeful Mrs Scott)* from the chemical ashes – minus hair, minus immune system and maybe, just maybe, minus the nasty wee bugger that's eating away not only at Hugh's 'lovely little cupcakes' but God knows which other parts of my sadly defeated body.

"Try knowing that the life you are whirling and

birling through could be cut short. Very short and very soon.

"And try lying here wondering if those forty odd years were all a waste of time and energy. If all that whirl was mindless and worthless. If your talents had been wasted and your potential unrealised."

'Don't upset yourself Anne. They mean well I'm sure.'

'If I survive this, I might just want to break free, run wild, think for myself and take risks. Be alive. That would shake them out of their precious little privileged existences.'

'Anne, hello. I'm in the hospital all morning and thought I'd just pop by. Can I pull up a chair or would you rather I came back later?'

The Rev Brian Kerr, bible in pocket, head tilted sympathetically, respectful of tone and almost apologetic in approach, tentatively reached for a visitor's chair.

'Oh it's good to see you Brian. Please sit down.'

'Now, how are we today, Anne? Bearing up?'

'Much the same. Just waiting and waiting. More tests. More results. You know how it is. But actually, I have been thinking about something and maybe you could help me, Brian.

'I want to raise some money for girls who have

little hope of ever having a life like I've had. It'll be something worthwhile to do if …' and she broke into a fit of coughing.

Holding her right hand on her abdomen, she caught her breath … 'if I don't make it. And even if I do, and perhaps especially if I do.

'Anyway, could you let me have some details of projects the church is supporting? And I'll look them over and see if there is some way I might get involved. Even in this pathetic state.'

She gestured at her wasted body.

Brian averted his gaze, busying himself extracting his diary from the inside pocket of his jacket. 'Oh what a very generous gesture. The Church of Scotland does missionary work all over the world. I'll bring you some information. We could look at it together on the computer, maybe later this week?

'Now is there anything else you'd like to discuss? Or maybe we could simply say a prayer together?

'No? No? Are you sure? Well, maybe not today. I'll just leave this leaflet here for you. *Words of encouragement* it says on the cover ... The Lord walks with you.'

'Ah -A mile in my shoes so to speak.'

She lay back down, breathing consciously and slowly.

After coffee time, she borrowed Gladys's laptop.

The Church of Scotland website proclaimed:

The aim of the World Mission Council is to enable the Church of Scotland to participate effectively in the Mission of God in the world, following the example and priorities of Jesus Christ and seeking the guidance of the Holy Spirit.

The World Mission Council seeks to fulfil that aim by:

Engaging in a process of attentive accompaniment with the Church of Scotland's partners worldwide. (That is, listening to and walking with our partners on our shared journey of faith)

Developing flexible models of partner-relationships and service opportunities with the world church

Maximising the available human and financial resources

Maximising the benefits to the Church in Scotland of involvement in the world church and communicating these benefits to the members and congregations of the Church of Scotland

Anne shook her head, slowly, muttering,

'Halleluiah for the jargon!'

She skipped most of that business speak, and looked at the photographic gallery.

A caption on the Malawi page caught her eye

After travelling only a short distance one begins passing

the giants. It is the valley of giants. Like a military guard they stand sentinel tall as they have been commissioned to guard the valley from unseen intruders. They are the giant stately baobab trees, and some have been standing here since before Christ walked the Judaea hills

The link took her to The Baobab Trust which sought to help young girls escape the fate of their gender.

HOW YOU CAN HELP

When the fundraising pack arrived it disgorged a host of golden ideas to raise funds to find foster homes for young girls to save them from teenage pregnancy and prostitution. A throng of suggestions. Sufficient loaves and fishes to feed the imagination of the dullest or least enthusiastic.

She picked up her notepad, used her rubber tipped pencil to scratch her bald head under the strategically tied headscarf, (blue spotted today to match her nightie), and applied her remaining energies to scoping out a plan of action to raise a hundred pounds for every year since her birth into a life of privilege.

Half an hour.

Then a rest.

Another visitor. More inanities.

Then another rest.

A meal – or what she could stomach of it. Then a brief nodding off.

Over several days, she addressed the task.

'What do you think of this Hugh?'

'What is it?'

'It's my *mission statement, outline strategy* and detailed *action plan* for the next three months – if I'm spared of course.'

'What on earth are you going on about, Anne? You're in a hospital, not the boardroom. And don't say *if I'm spared.* We're trying to remain optimistic, remember?'

'Oh, optimistic, realistic, pessimistic. What will be, will be Hugh. And this might be my last chance to do something worthwhile with my life. So listen for once, will you please?

'Mission statement: to raise £5000 to support the Baobab Trust in the provision of foster homes for teenage girls in Malawi.

'Strategic plan: to involve friends, family and all who offer to *help in any way we can Anne; you just need to ask.*

Stop for a minute to get breath back.

Action statement: three pronged programme of fund raising. Namely:

A West End cocktail party in aid of the Baobab Trust – to be organised by residents of Murrayfield Avenue. *Now they'll know what 'busy' and 'social whirl' are for.*

Obs and gynae department sponsored car rally – *might as well put these fancy cars to some use instead of just being dick-extensions – and that's your bit Hugh.*

Give it up for charity – auction of precious pieces – *to be organised by Simone. She's the arty one among us. And you can start by giving her that Gypsy Girl figure. I never liked it.*

'That sounds ...'

'Shh. Wait. I'm not finished.'

'And of course one final piece of action will be to ask for donations at my funeral.'

'Anne, for goodness sake. Please don't talk like that. We're not thinking along those lines. The doctors have said they are hopeful.'

'Hopeful. But no guarantees. And I've had all the chemo I can have. There's nothing else now except good luck or miracles.

'Anyway, if it keeps me happy it's the least you can do. I'm not asking for much. I could be like Annie who went home last week. She was badgering her husband for a new sports car. *It's the last car you'll ever have to buy me darling.* What could he say?

'I'm relying on you to help me Hugh. You'll need to be my mouthpiece outside of this room. That's not normally a problem for you my love, is it?'

With that, she lay back on the pillows, as if suddenly completely exhausted.

Hugh kissed her briefly on the cheek.

'Chin up dear. I'm right on to it. Reporting back at fourteen hundred hours tomorrow, sah!'

With a mock salute he clicked his heels, about-turned, and walked quickly out of the side room and past the nurses' station on his way to the lift.

He brushed past her named nurse, pre-occupied with the thought of fund raising, wondering where he'd garner the enthusiasm and drive.

But of one thing he was in no doubt. The *Gypsy Girl* was staying. 'She' wasn't going anywhere.

The West End cocktail party went ahead without its chief fundraiser who was confined to bed at home with a chest infection, which would precipitate a return to the hospital for intravenous anti-biotic treatment.

The sponsored car rally was taking some time to organise, given the need for numerous health and safety measures to be drawn up.

Simone was using up copious amounts of A4, drafting and redrafting plans for the Give It Up For Charity event. Organisational abilities being latent in the underused left hand side of her brain.

Anne's sudden death – a shattering blow to all some six weeks later – gave rise to a certain covert relief that fund raising plans might now need to be 'modified'.

Hugh and Simone were individually adamant that they would each continue to work for the charity in a way that befitted Anne's memory – after a suitable time of mourning of course

Altered state

Edinburgh February 2010

Mabel phoned the next day. She sounded agitated and spoke at speed as if not to draw breath.

'I know you'll be busy with all the arrangements for the … em ... Friday isn't it? But I just thought, seeing as you'll no doubt be having people back after the … the event, you'll be needing the house spotless. Just the way Mrs Scott always had it.' She sighed with audible relief at having jumped that awkward hurdle.

'So I thought I would come round all day Wednesday and make everything just so. One less thing for you to worry about.' She was back in control.

There was silence on the other end. Hugh hesitated, as he attempted to gather his thoughts, something he was finding increasingly difficult to do in the almost constant fog which swirled around in his head. 'Eh, yes. Oh yes, Mabel. Yes indeed. Very thoughtful of you. Yes, very. Wednesday was it?' He panicked slightly. *What was happening on Wednesday?*

'I might not be in but I'm sure you know your way round better than I do, after all these years. Emily might be here too. Thank you, thanks. I hadn't quite got round to thinking about all that. But yes, we'll want the place ship shape.'

Earlier that morning, Hugh had struggled to remain focussed when he went to St Peter's Church in Corstorphine Road to meet up with the Minister. He'd left the children in their respective beds, Emily with the duvet drawn right up around her neck and the top sheet pulled across her mouth as if holding in her thoughts, and Andrew, bed linen resembling the beach after a storm, wreckage from a night of tossing and turning on the waves of nightmares. They seemed to operate in a different time zone from his own and were both oblivious to his gaze as he checked for their breathing, something he'd last done in a different world, in a long forgotten time.

He'd gone armed with the titles of the very few hymns their collective memories could dredge up. *For the beauty of the earth. One more step along the world I go. Jesus loves me, this I know.* Memories from school assemblies, scout flag dedication ceremonies, family Christenings. The only funereal title they were familiar with was *Abide with me,* and Anne had always hated that hymn. Enough to make the whole congregation slit their wrists, she'd said.

The decisions had to be made that day in time for the hymn sheets to be printed. It was one more item to check off that list and hope you get right.

The Reverend Kerr stood at the open door of the manse. 'Come in Dr Scott, do come in. Thank you for popping by. It's always better to talk in situ if you get my drift. We can walk through how events will proceed on the day that much more easily.

'Can I first say that if there is anything I can do, now and at any other time, for you and your family, please just ask? I got to know Anne very well during my visits to the hospital. I can imagine she is a huge loss to you all. Now a cup of tea maybe before we get down to it?'

Hugh sat down in the well-worn armchair. 'Thank you but no. Maybe later. I'm conscious of your time too. Now about the order of service ...'

'Ah yes. As you'll no doubt be aware, Anne had made a selection of her favourites. I have the list here. We'll have to narrow down the number, however. Maybe you'd like five minutes to look them over again and choose four.'

Hugh crushed his oh-so inappropriate list into a crumpled ball in his pocket. Would there be other surprises?

They agreed Andrew would do a reading. As would

Alan. The standard ones – from first Corinthians, chapter 13

If I speak in the tongues of men and of angels, but have not love, I am only a resounding gong or a clanging cymbal…

And John 14

Let not your heart be troubled: ye believe in God, believe also in me. In my Father's house are many mansions: if it were not so, I would have told you. I go to prepare a place for you …

There would be a retiring collection for The Baobab Trust in Malawi. The minister would remind the congregation that they were invited to join the family for a cup of tea in the Murrayfield Hotel afterwards. Hugh and the family would greet mourners at the front door on the way out.

'And lastly, I just need to confirm with you that you still want the Rancman poem to grace the back cover of the hymn sheet. As you know, Anne had great faith that she was on a journey that was far from over. She often quoted it to me in the final weeks. It's one of my personal favourites too.'

He quoted from memory.

When I come to the end of the road
And the sun has set for me,
I want no rites in a gloom filled room
Why cry for a soul set free!
Miss me a little, but not for long,
And not with your head bowed low.
Remember the love we once shared,

Miss me, but let me go!
For this a journey we all must take,
And each must go alone;
It's all a part of the master's plan
A step on the road to home.
When you are lonely and sick of heart
Go to the friends we know,
And bury your sorrows in doing good deeds,
Miss me, but let me go.

Hugh would have to look that one up on Google. Whew. She'd obviously had the discussions. Only not with him.

'Don't worry Dr Scott. I'll put all this in an email to you. The wonders of modern technology – even in the church these days. The undertaker will take care of the printing. All will be in place for Friday. Will we just say a few words in prayer before now you go?'

Hugh had opted for 'a celebration of Anne's life' on the intimation. But when it came to the day, the voices in his head whispered *'What about me? What about me? What's going to happen to me now?'*

Even after standing with face presented under a long, piping hot shower, and gulping down two cups of strong, black coffee, Hugh still had the imprint of a heavy night's drinking on his face. A hint of puffiness under the eyes, a trace of yellow in the sclera, a few beads of perspiration on his forehead. But *what else would anyone expect of the grieving spouse?* he reasoned. Breathing in, he lengthened his spine to attain his full height, tucked his chin slightly under to counteract his natural tendency to lead from the front, and judged himself ready to go.

With an awkward hug for his in-laws, Hugh gathered the children and Anne's parents together in the sitting room before the funeral cars arrived. Emily in a short black dress with a grey and black striped jacket, Andrew in a new blue suit, the crispness of his white shirt collar causing a red rash around his neck. Jane Fotheringham in navy with a matching hat, dabbed her powdered nose with a delicate lace-edged handkerchief. Husband James blinked repeatedly.

Having checked in the oval mirror that his Windsor knot was perfect, Hugh coughed twice. 'This will be a very hard day for all of us. But we'll do Anne credit if we remain dignified and in control. There'll be plenty of time for tears at the private burial later. We'll be on our own then and at liberty to give in to grief if we want to. So let's all go chin up and do what has to be done, okay?'

The grandparents took charge of the two young adults, their usual confident sophisticated patina threatening to crack and splinter.

Hugh travelled with Anne. One last journey. Hugh and Anne. Anne and Hugh. For one last time.

And then? ... another tear in the fabric of his life. Another hitch in the plan. Another shift in the bedrock.

What was that quote? *Miss me but let me go?*

But what about me? What about me? was all he could think.

Standing at the front, in the pew labelled 'Chief Mourners only please' Hugh held himself together, focussing on the stained glass windows, the various commemorative wall plaques honouring long-dead 'ministers of this parish' and the tattered flags of old, now disbanded regiments who'd fought and died for the noble cause.

Emily had to whisper to him on more than one occasion that he should sit down or stand up. He turned to comment once or twice to Anne on elements of the service, as if a bystander in his own life.

Jane reminded him to leave the single white lily on Anne's coffin which would remain in front of the altar till the mourners had left.

The incongruous bright sunlight beating down on the church steps seemed to jolt him back to reality.

'A lovely lady. So gracious.'

'And only fifty-two. Life just isn't fair.'

'You must so be so proud of your children, Hugh.

Emily, beautiful, just like her Mother. Andrew, upright and smart. Both so brave.'

Hugh's left fist was clenched tight by his side, as he shook hands with the never-ending procession, his nails digging into his palms to keep the emotions at bay. An occasional hug was harder to handle.

Colleagues patted his shoulder.

'Don't hurry back, Hugh. Take all the time you need. There are no short-cuts to grieving remember.'

'We doctors are only human, Hugh, even though we don't always act like it.'

No mention was made of his other 'problems'. And if some of them were hazy on dates and opted to link his 'unfortunate lapse into inappropriate behaviour with Christine' with his obvious upset over Anne's illness (*didn't someone say he nearly had a breakdown*?), then so be it.

Alan approached with pursed lips, shaking his head.

Hugh took his outstretched hand in both of his. 'Thanks Alan. You hit just the right note with that reading. I'm not exactly religious as you know. But sometimes the Bible can be very comforting.'

'We'll see you at the hotel,' was all Alan could manage, the words caught in his throat as he stifled his grief.

Simone gave him a quick hug, her handkerchief

over her mouth and nose. He caught a whispered 'Que Dieu te bénisse – God bless you.'

And with an involuntary sniff and shiver, she followed her husband and son to the car park.

The tea was somewhat stewed by the time everyone sat down. And the hotel had to be reminded to provide herbal alternatives. The sausage rolls finally arrived when the guests at some tables had already started on the cakes.

It all passed Hugh by.

Handshakes, kind words, another dram to help you drown your sorrows. *Sit here and I'll get you a plate of sandwiches Dad. You'd better eat something.* All was played out in a haze.

'What about me? What will I do now?'

Andrew and Emily stayed to see off the last few lingering guests, who had long moved on from reminiscing about Anne to discussing rugby scores, the state of the Stock Market and the best place in Edinburgh to buy extra virgin olive oil *from authentic sources.* Luc helped them pick up the discarded hymn sheets to take home, rather than just leave them for the waiting staff to put in the recycle bin like so much scrap paper.

Alan and Simone drove Hugh home, his Windsor knot long undone, his gait unsteady, his head somewhat bowed.

'Come on Hugh. Let's get you home now. You've done your bit for today.'

Hugh slumped into the nearest armchair, exhausted and beaten. Lifting an arm of leaden weight, he waved his hand in the approximate direction of the kitchen.

'Coffee if you want it. In the kitchen. You'll find it. All there.'

Simone went to investigate while Alan helped Hugh undo the knots in his laces and remove his black shoes.

'Okay, old chum. Take it easy. That's it done. Don't worry about a thing now.'

'Whisky. That's what we need, Alan. A dram. Glenfiddich in the drinks cupboard. Plenty of it. *One for my baby and one more for the road.*'

'Let's have a coffee first. Plenty time for a dram later.'

'Live a little, you old fart. Have a whisky. Who needs sodding coffee at a time like this?' Hugh's voice became animated with a false sense of gaiety. He was on his feet making for the drinks cupboard.

'Anne, Anne! Get some ice for these whiskies will you?'

Alan put an arm round Hugh's shoulder, and guided him back to his chair, as his friend stumbled and staggered, tears now blinding his eyes as he remembered as if for the first time what had befallen Anne.

'She's gone Hugh. And now we need to look after you. Help you get your life back together. Have a cup of coffee with us, and then we'll see what comes next.'

Simone appeared with a cafetière, china mugs and a plate of cherry cake on a tray.

'Ah, the beautiful Simone. Will you share her with me, Alan? Remember that blood brothers stuff from years ago? *A bond never to be broken and what's mine is yours.* Come and sit beside me Simone. Let me feast on your loveliness.' He doffed his imaginary hat as if in homage.

Simone looked questioningly to Alan who shrugged as if to say, 'humour him for now.'

She sat down gingerly on the well-padded arm of the brown leather chair, perched like a bird ready to fly off at the slightest movement. A silver photograph frame on the adjacent mantelpiece caught her attention. Anne with uncharacteristic wind-blown hair, walking along a beach, laughing at something an unseen companion might have said to amuse her.

'Where was that photograph taken Hugh? She looks so beautiful and carefree.'

Hugh's coffee remained untouched as he began to reminisce. As if in a world of his own, he travelled back through time, remembering where they'd been, how she'd looked, what she'd said.

Simone stroked his left hand all the while as if to reassure him that they were listening. Alan and Simone exchanged pensive smiles.

Hugh went quiet. And then as if struck by a sudden flash of white lightning, sat up straight and shouted to no-one and everyone, 'And what did I do? What did I do? What did this rotten son-of-a-bitch do to his loyal, caring, beautiful wife?

'I' – as he placed his right hand over his heart space – 'I hardly acknowledged she was there. I took her presence for granted every day of our married life. And when she found out about the others, she didn't make a fuss. She … simply… withdrew... her heart … from me.' He began to sob, catching his breath as he struggled to remain a man.

Simone shook her head and put a finger to his lips, whispering 'Non. Non. Don't be so hard on yourself. She loved you till the day she died.'

Brushing her aside, he suddenly stood up tall and as if speaking to an audience, imitating the earnest, well-meaning Presbyterian minister of earlier in the day, he orated, 'Love one another. Never do harm. What God has joined together, let no man put asunder!'

And with a finger pointed at Simone, he left them with 'and *you* remember that – always!' as he headed for the sitting room door, fumbling with the handle before lurching off in the direction of the staircase to the upstairs bedrooms.

Simone busied herself tidying up, righting the chair cushions, polishing the leather arm where she'd been sitting, with the sleeve of her black woollen cardigan. Alan watched her as she worked, seemingly avoiding his eyes.

'What did you think of that?'

'I think we wait ten minutes and then we leave, Alain. Long enough to make sure he is safely asleep. Poor lamb. All those mixed-up thoughts and memories.'

Alan was at the bottom of the stairs ready to make a final check on his old friend when Emily, Andrew and Luc appeared through the front door.

'You look shattered Dad. I'm going to stay here with the others tonight if that's okay. We'll take care of Uncle Hugh. How is he?'

Simone cut in quickly 'He's needing rest. Too much of the whisky. It's affecting his memory. Everything is confused for him. You stay Luc, that's good. I'll take Papa home.'

As Alan flossed his teeth some half an hour later, he remarked to his wife as she brushed her long dark hair, and examined the crows' feet beneath her newly cleansed eyes, 'they certainly make you think. Funerals. Maybe you see some things in a different light all of a sudden.'

'Mmm. Always a sad day.'

'And what do you think he meant about sharing you with him?'

'Oh that was just the drink talking Alain. He won't remember any of that tomorrow, and if he does, he'll be – what do you say – mortified. Yes – mortified.'

'You know, he's been a bad boy over the years. Cheated on Anne. That bit was true. I wonder what he'll choose once he realises that he really is free to do what he wants now.'

'Oh, he'll probably find a nice Edinburgh lady to take her place. But not yet. Not for a while. And we need to be there for him while he adapts to the changes in his life.'

'Just be aware Simone. That's all. Don't get too close. He's my best pal, but you're a beautiful enigmatic woman with a deep soul. That's very attractive to many men. And he'll be vulnerable.'

'What do you mean – that I would entice him? What are you trying to say, Alain? Or that another man could tempt me away? Is that it? Don't you trust me? What have I ever done to make you think like that? Nothing! That's what! You've hurt me, now. You really have. I'm going to bed!'

She didn't remove her silk nightgown when she slid between the covers, but gathered the sheets around her as if to make an impenetrable shield. Her breathing had returned to normal only by the time Alan returned from making his final checks on the house.

'Simone?' he whispered as he tried to put an arm around her. 'Simone. I'm sorry. I am so sorry. My biggest fear is that you leave me for someone else. I see men look at you and can read their minds. They think, "who is that exotic beauty? Who is that free spirit?" You're different. You're not like Scottish women. You have a hint of mystery; your eyes can be hypnotic. You're ...'

'Stop exaggerating, Alain. I am a fifty-three year old woman, married for nearly thirty years to the man I chose for life. And anyway, I'm ageing. My beauty is slowly disappearing. Can't you see it happening?'

'You'll always be beautiful to me, always. Just remember how much I love you and please forgive me when I don't live up to your expectations.'

She relaxed her foetal position, moved on to her back and took hold of his hand. 'Alain. I have been with you for most of my adult life. I wouldn't know how to live without you. So please – let's stop this kind of talk. I'll be a friend to Hugh if he needs me. But that will be all. Okay?'

'Okay, sorry, sorry.'

As he turned on to his left side, she followed, moulding herself around his broad back. 'Now,' she whispered as she lightly kissed his shoulder. 'Let me see if I can reassure you.' She slipped out of her nightdress

Her best efforts produced a disappointing result. He quietly removed her hand, kissed it and held it to his chest.

'I don't want to let you down,' he said with a slight tremble in his voice.

'Don't worry. It's been a long emotional day. There'll be many tomorrows.'

She turned away from him to switch out the bedside light. He waited for her to turn back. *How long would she put up with it?*

May cause depression

Musselburgh, April 2011

She collapses wearily onto the front doorstep, swivelling sideways and backwards, allowing her weight to push the door all the way back until it comes to rest against the porch wall.

It isn't as warm outside as she'd imagined earlier, when looking out through the dining room window at the midday sky. She should have brought a cushion to sit on, and a cardigan to wrap around her shoulders. Too late now for that, she doesn't intend moving again for a while; it has been enough of an effort getting this far. The April sun is shining brightly, although its power is weakened by a pulsating wind that swirls and ebbs all around her, and through her, causing the inside door to rattle with each new surge of air.

She pushes her sleeves up, so as to expose more skin, and better feel the wind's energy, capturing what warmth there is available on her bare arms. Sitting sideways like this, with one leg inside and the other outside, she can just manage to keep her skin from erupting into goose bumps; and if she shuts her eyes and surrenders to the rhythms she can almost convince herself she is back in Montpelier again.

The wind is growing stronger now, lifting her hair up in small clumps, blasting it in the manner of a dryer on full volume, then depositing it back on her scalp in random fashion, only to pick up another clump from elsewhere and do the same with that.

She catches a glimpse of her reflection in the glass panes of the inner door and doesn't quite recognise herself. Her hair, naturally wavy, is now even more tousled than usual; wild, strong, blowing aimlessly in every direction. She looks a mess. But there are worse things. As she draws her bare legs up and clasps her arms around them she feels the unmistakable rub of stubble against her wrists. Her lip curls up on one side and an involuntary grunt escapes from deep in her body. She is ashamed of herself, the state of her legs, her own laziness. She's slipping.

Drawing a packet of cigarettes from her shirt pocket she places one in her mouth, then fishes around for the lighter which her fingers can't locate. It must be on the kitchen table still. She closes her eyes and at the same time takes a deep breath in an attempt to stay calm. Then she tries to refocus into the feelings of the rippling sensations along her arms, and the air massaging her face. It's in vain. The little joy she felt from the warmth in the air is now rapidly evaporating. She knows she will have to get back to work before this mood settles and darkens.

Turning her head towards the garden, her gaze falls on the old tree that dominates the corner near the road. The branches are swaying gently, their leaves furled with the promise of openings to come. Except on the one dead branch, which is fractured – lightening damaged by the look of it – its bark gone. Exposed to the elements with no protection, the wood has become pale and scarred. How long has it been like that, she wonders? Why hasn't Alain cut it off? Hasn't he noticed how it spoils the appearance of the tree?

She sighs, deeply, forcing the air out of her mouth in a rushing sound. Of course he hasn't noticed. What *does* he notice these days? And even if he had, so what? He doesn't care about imperfection now does he? Not even in himself. Not enough to *do* anything about it. Not even for her. When did he stop caring? She must have blinked and missed it – for certainly she is unable to pin it down to any given point in recent time.

She stares at the tree again, feeling some affinity with its predicament. She has a dead branch too, but it is inside her, where no-one can see it. She's taken care to hide it from the world, away from prying eyes. She would chop it out if that were possible, but she's afraid to try, in case she can't cope with the pain. Yet if she doesn't get rid of it, will its lifelessness spread like a numbing disease and result in a death by slow paralysis?

She tires of the introspection; turns her neck first one way, then the other, straightens her knees, smoothes her skirt down and pulls herself up using the door handle. She will go and find the lighter, have the cigarette, pick up her chisel and then get back to the figure. With her sculpture at least, she is still able to turn something inert into an object with edges, with curves, with expression, with movement. Into an object that has life.

Alternative therapy

Musselburgh, September the same year

As Alan nudged open their bedroom door with his foot, Simone's right arm emerged from the storm tossed sea of bedding in anticipation of that first cup of the day.

'Hot and strong. Mmm. That's good.'

After several sips, she placed the blue china mug carefully on top of the coaster on the bedside table.

Then pushing her hair back out of her eyes and massaging her cheeks with her fingertips, she asked Alan, 'Will you be back at the usual time, my love?'

'**I wish**. LMC meeting tonight. Usual stuff' – and he listed them one by one on his fingers –'changes to pensions, problems with secondary care discharge letters, lack of parking on health board premises. Would you like to go in my place? It is so much fun I could cry.'

He knotted his scarf with an angry flourish, picked up his briefcase and headed for the bedroom door.

Simone touched his arm as he passed. 'Ah if only there was something I *could* do to lighten that load you carry on those broad shoulders, I would gladly do it. That was another restless night you had.'

With a grim look he answered 'Well, you can tidy up the garden if you want. Wash out last year's planters; rake any old leaves out of the borders, even up the edges before the grass starts growing. How about that, eh?'

She pouted and shrugged her shoulders.

'That wasn't really what I had in mind Alain. But maybe we could do some work in the garden together at the weekend. Then go out for a nice dinner afterwards?'

'Aye maybe. We'll see. It'll probably rain. Anyway, don't wait up for me.'

The front door banged shortly afterwards. She lay back and exhaled a long slow breath.

Whatever was the matter with Alain, nothing she suggested seemed to be the answer.

Maybe she was part of the problem. Cooking wasn't her strong point. Nor housework. That hadn't mattered when they were first married. And then when Luc was born, Alain was so besotted with his boy that he'd have done anything for the woman who had given birth to him.

Once Luc had gone to school, Simone had assumed the full-time role of the artist, the slightly eccentric Frenchwoman with the tumbling curls and bohemian clothes. She knew it gave Alain some degree of extra status to be married to this unusual wife. He would exaggerate the pronunciation of her name, Simone Fournier-Fraser, giving full rein to his French accent. And he'd never criticised her Gallic instincts or attitudes. Or asked her to change in any way. But maybe he wanted something different now.

Maybe she'd taken him for granted. Gone to bed early leaving him sitting up late watching movies all on his own. Placed Luc in his reliable care to go shopping or visit exhibitions at the weekends.

She'd stopped trying. She could see that now.

Worn woolly socks in bed on those freezing winter nights when the east wind blowing off the North Sea found every slither of a gap in the fabric of their old house.

Gone without any make-up when she was absorbed in the design of a piece for her latest collection. Let her hair go an extra day without washing to escape a draughty bathroom on a winter morning.

Yes, that must be it. He didn't find her interesting or arousing any more. A new Simone was needed. New attitudes, new looks. Rejuvenation. A sudden energy lifted her spirits, strengthened her will, focussed her mind and propelled her forward…in the direction of Jenners.

Our personal stylists can help create a new you. Discover your true essence and maximise its fragrance and impact. Hair, make up and wardrobe advice. Discreet and individually tailored to meet your needs.

But first the customer questionnaire.

'What is all *this*?' Simone asked of Shelley, standing there all pert and young and smart in her Phase 8 dress. 'Do I prefer the east wind or the west wind? Am I happier beside the sea? I don't understand. Why all these questions?'

She threw her hands up in mock exasperation and leaned closer to Shelley.

'All you need to know is that my husband is under a lot of stress at the moment, and I want to be the best I can be to help him. And that means attractive, youthful, interesting to talk to, encouraging, more loving.

'Now can you help me get rid of these crows' feet? And maybe change my hair in some way. Look, here is a photograph of me ten years ago. I want to look like that again. You understand?'

Shelley had the sense to hold out her hand to take back the *Holistic You* questionnaire, with a reference to 'some of our clients like a more touchy-feely approach, Mrs Fraser. But I can see you know exactly what you want. And that's so refreshing. Shall we go down to the cosmetics department first?'

A glass of French Red would have complemented

the light lunch admirably – and didn't these girls realise how good it was for the skin? A minor point as it turned out. Five hours after arriving, Simone looked in every mirror she passed between the personal shoppers' private cash desk on the third floor and the front exit on Princes Street, unable to quite believe in the young-ish, shiny haired, lissom figure who met her gaze.

The bill, neatly folded and concealed in a tasteful cream and brown edged envelope, detailed the costs of:

- several items of new shape-giving underwear
- a range of skin care products for mature skin including a 100% Organic Grape Water
- a restyle, cut and colour by Angus of Hair by Design, with one of his complimentary miracle shampoo preparations thrown in
- a tapestry covered pocket sized book of swatches of material, the product of colour analysis
- a turquoise silk shirt and a pair of silver capri pants

All for the not so reasonable sum of ...Well, the cost didn't really matter.

Simone, denying her instinct to act on impulse and book the first available appointment, had arranged her makeover for a Wednesday which was Alan's half day. He was usually home by 3pm, and not just as world weary or bad humoured as on other working days.

His car was already in the drive when she arrived home.

She slipped into the downstairs loo to check that her hair was still in place, and to refresh her lipstick, noting with some satisfaction that the cold breeze had heightened the colour in her cheeks.

'Alain. Darling I'm home. Where are you?'

She finally found him in the garden shed, sorting out those planters, apparently unable to wait till they might do it together. Cursing when one empty plant pot became jammed inside another. Kicking a rake that fell over and landed in his path. And apparently reliving a consultation from earlier in the day. Playing both parts with word and action.

'Well, Mrs *I've Been on the Internet* – maybe you would like to swap places with me today?' Gesturing to an imaginary seat.

'Yes – I mean it. Sit there and let me tell you *my* symptoms for a change. Jaded, tired, grumpy, feeling old, experiencing no pleasure in life. Yes, that's me. Your friendly family doctor. Oh and don't forget ED.

'What's ED? WHAT IS ED? Come on now. Surely you know that? Erectile dysfunction to medical people like you and me. Or would you prefer the vernacular? Can't get it up. Can't keep it up. No lead in the pencil any more. Get my drift?

'And Mrs Know it all – what would you suggest? *A few wee pills maybe. They blue anes aff the internet. You can only get wan a week if the doactor prescribes them. And that won't keep the wife at hame will it? She'll be aff quick as a flash.'*

Simone crept back towards the house.

This situation was worse than she had imagined. A makeover wouldn't be enough.

The evening ended as many had in previous weeks, with Alan saying 'sorry love, I'm just too tired tonight' and Simone replying 'of course you are, of course you are. Let's wait for the weekend.'

The weekends came and went.

A few weeks later, as Simone left the underground car park, the sun was shining, the castle standing proud, the flags of Scotland, the United Kingdom and the EU fluttering above the shopping plaza, and Simone's spirits were momentarily uplifted by the unfailing splendour of Ramsay Court, high above Princes Street.

As she hastened towards the National Gallery of Scotland where she wanted to check out Canova's sculpture 'The Three Graces', her mind already on her next project, she felt a hand on her left arm.

Whirling round in surprise, she was met with a light kiss and a smile from Hugh.

'Slow down pretty lady. You're too quick for me!'

'Ah Hugh. I am just on my way to see The Three Graces, looking for inspiration. As usual my mind was elsewhere. How are you?'

They walked together towards the Mound.

'Why don't I come with you, then we can have coffee and a chat after you see your bit of sculpture?'

'That *bit of sculpture* is one of the most beautiful works of art ever created!'

'I know, I know. Just like you, my dear Simone. Now take me there so I can compare thee to it, and find it wanting next to your classic beauty!'

Hugh wandered round as Simone studied the piece from all angles. Imagining running her hand down the smooth line of the back of Thalia, she felt a fleeting pang of loss. Once Alain would have enjoyed her smooth skin, would have kissed the nape of her neck, murmured his love for her and made her feel completely special and treasured. Her breath caught in her throat.

'Ok Simone? Is everything ok?

It had never been her intention to raise the subject of Alan's problem. Hugh had sensed her sadness, probed with a clinician's skill for the causes and she'd crumpled.

'Don't tell him Hugh. Please. He'd be furious. And anyway, we should be talking about you, and how you are bearing up.'

'Oh I'm a survivor Simone. You know that better than most. And you are too. You and I – we're the same. We always pull through in the end.'

He responded to her quizzical look with, 'You know, we could help each other. I'm a bit lonely. You're needing some attention. We could meet up once a week. Coffee, a chat. Maybe more if you felt like it. We've always been good together, you and me.'

'Hugh, that was in the past. What are you thinking about? Whatever happened before was impulsive, silly, risky. I love Alain and I am not making a plan to have a secret life. I don't know how you can even think like that.'

Hugh leaned in closer, caught her by the arm, pulled her towards him, whispered in her ear, 'I know you have your needs. Don't deny it, my Gypsy Girl. And don't deny that I can satisfy them. Think about it. No-one need ever know.'

As she wrenched her arm free, and looked frantically in all directions to find the exit, he called after her: 'Phone me Simone. I'll be waiting for your call.'

An Open Wound

Musselburgh October

Dr Fraser consulted impatiently the new telephone list on the wall adjacent to his desk. *Could nothing stay the same for five minutes?* Peering over his glasses he looked for Isobel's new number. Practice Manager – 661. She'd better be in.

She answered promptly. 'Dr Fraser – what can I do for you?'

'That appointment in my diary for Tuesday afternoon at 4 o'clock? That's usually the time I do my paperwork isn't it? And what's GEEPCAT when it's at home?'

She sighed wearily. 'Don't you remember? We agreed to take part in a research project into practice teamwork and communication. GEEPCAT it's called. We thought it would help us when we apply for the LES in Management of Depression. Someone called Miranda Hallhead from Glasgow Caledonian is coming to interview you on Wednesday.'

'Why me?'

'Oh it's not just you, Dr Fraser. She'll be seeing us all over the next week at one time or another. And anyway, it'll only take half an hour, she said.'

'Well, that's all she'll get from me,' he said sharply, slamming the drawer of his desk shut. 'I can't imagine why I agreed to it in the first place. We've got enough to do without some bloody intrusive researcher taking up our valuable time.'

Isobel rolled her eyes and spoke deliberately. 'If you remember, you were there at the meeting when it was discussed, although it *is* some time ago. 20th February I think. You'll find the minutes in the folder called …'

As if we ever read the minutes. 'Okay, okay. I'll do it, I'll do it. Just don't give me any other surprises this week will you? Life's busy enough. I've got the Ethics Committee meeting on Thursday and my peer assessment on Friday afternoon. Some week this is turning out to be.'

The following Wednesday, Alan switched off his voice recorder to answer the knock at his surgery door, and with a hint of a sigh responded with a 'Yes?'

It was Isobel. 'Miss Miranda Hallhead to see you Dr Fraser. I'll hold all calls for the next half hour.'

'Come in, come in. Don't hang back. Time's in very

short supply, Miss Hallhead.'

With a warning finger, and a look as if to say 'behave,' Isobel shut the door behind her.

The young dark-haired researcher sat down as invited, on the plastic covered upright chair placed at such an angle as to allow the doctor to create the desired non-confrontational relationship with his patient. She took out her notebook and pen from her oversized black handbag, pulled up her chair and began to recite her standard preamble.

'Thank you for seeing me Dr Fraser. I appreciate that you are very busy and promise that I won't take up any more of your time than necessary. Can I just start by reminding you of the purpose of this interview, and what you can expect during the next half hour?'

He nodded his head and gave her a half-smile. 'Fine, fine. Keep it brief.'

A full five minutes passed in aims and objectives, sampling techniques, outcomes, assurances of anonymity, and collection of basic data – name, age, date of qualification, years in general practice. All the while, Alan's left leg was jiggling and his foot tapping underneath his desk.

He was accustomed to *quantitative* research – yes or no, rank in order, rate from 1 to 5, all followed by number crunching of some kind. Data in, computer calculates, statistics out. As a result, he was momentarily thrown by her first proper research question. 'In your own words, what is it like to work here?'

He looked to her in puzzlement for guidance – 'well, I don't know what you're getting at. It's a health centre. I'm a doctor. What else is there to say?'

'I'm interested in how you *feel* about working here.'

He looked at her with disbelief, his bushy eyebrows just about meeting in the middle.

'How I *feel* about it? Well how would you feel if you'd been thirty odd years a doctor and were running out of energy and patience?'

She'd had all kinds of reactions to this question, and knew just what to say.

'It's not my job to make assumptions Dr Fraser. I'd just like you to give me your instant response without thinking too much about it. There are no right or wrong answers.'

Alan blew out through his cheeks. 'I tell you what. How about I tell you what I like and what I don't like about the job and you can cobble it together from that?'

'That's fine. Please go ahead.'

'I'll start with what I don't like. That's the longer list.' He smiled wanly, running his fingers through his hair.

Miranda might as well have thrown her interview schedule with its list of open questions such as 'how do people get on in this practice?' and 'what works well here?' over her shoulder, as once Alan started there was no stopping him. He missed no-one in his list of idiots and incompetents, painted his partners as a shower of lazy dodgers, railed against the modern NHS with its bean counters, thought police and cross infection Gestapo and bemoaned the passing of the days when doctors were accorded due respect from patients, and played golf on Wednesday afternoons.

As he wiped his brow at what she interpreted as the end of his response, Miranda pondered whether to bother prompting him as to what he *did* like. With one eye on the surgery clock, she opted instead to ask her customary catch-all final question from her intended list – 'and is there anything else you would like to add?'

'Find another job, lassie. Or they'll get you too in the end.'

And with that, he opened the door and made to usher her out.

Alan noted that the front door of his house was wide-open as he drove up. A strong wind was threatening to slam it shut before he reached it. He pulled it behind him, double locking it to make extra sure.

'Simone? Luc? Where the devil is everyone? We could have been burgled by now. The flat screen TV, the computer, the whole bloody lot!' He strode through the family room to the kitchen, took the stairs two at a time, flung open bedroom doors, pulled back bedcovers, all the while shouting as he went, 'you might as well invite them all in for a cup of tea. Make it easy for them why don't you! Do you think I work till I drop to let it all go into the back of a lorry bound for Leith backstreets?'

Simone wandered into the kitchen from her garden studio, hair in disarray as if she had been tearing it out in some kind of creative frustration, artist's apron bearing the marks of her hastily wiped hands.

'Ah Alain. I thought I heard you. How was your day?'

He grabbed her by the arms, as she was advancing to give him a hug. Roughly, he spun her round and marched her through to the front hallway.

Shocked, she blurted out, 'You're hurting me, Alain. Stop it, please.'

He didn't let her go.

'And *you're* hurting *me*!' he shouted, 'leaving the front door open like that. Who knows what might have happened? I'm sick of telling you to pay attention to safety and security! You turn off the night sensor light by mistake, you forget to shut the kitchen window when you go out, you leave the safe open when you take out your rings, and you don't set the alarm when you 'pop out to the shops.

'It's a BIG, BAD world out there Simone. Don't you understand? There are plenty of people who would like to cut us down, steal our hard earned possessions, destroy our home. So don't leave the bloody front door open – ever again!'

'I don't know what you mean Alain. Who are these bad people? Where are they? What do they want with us? You're frightening me. Please let me go.'

He pushed her away roughly, and wagged a finger at her.

'I told you before. They're everywhere. They see what we have and they want it. If they can't earn it themselves, they'll take it wherever they find it. And not only our possessions. Our position, our jobs. No-one is safe. Not even doctors! Research projects, significant event analyses, GP appraisal – those are just other names for finding us wanting and using that evidence to break up the current system. Get rid of GPs. That's what they want. Bring in nurses to do what we do. It's started already. Nurse-led clinics. Nurses staffing out- of-hours centres. NHS 24 calls answered by nurses. For Christ's sake, we've even got it in our practice – nurse-bloody-triage. I'll fight the bastards to the death if they try to get us out!'

He was shaking, florid, wide-eyed, frightening. He stumbled as if avoiding cobwebs in a dark cave, pushing a way through with his hands to the downstairs loo. Simone watched him go, swithering whether she should follow or maintain a safe distance.

Luc found her some minutes later curled up in the big armchair, arms in a pose of self-protection, eyes squeezed shut, breathing erratically.

'Did … you … remember … to lock the … front door Luc? Please check. Please. Do it now!'

'Chill out Simone. What's the deal? It's shut and I'll lock it later. It's only 6 o'clock. No tattie bogles out at this time.'

'No. Do it now. And from now on always do it when you come in. There are bad men out there. Your Papa told me.'

Luc kissed his mother on the forehead, 'Don't listen to him. He's exaggerating as usual. But I'll do it if it makes you feel better. Where is the old man anyway?'

Alan called them both through to the hallway some time later. Notebook in hand he demonstrated the new code for the burglar alarm. He'd deliberated for some considerable time to find a suitable four digit number. Something that no intruder would guess but which would be easy for them to remember. Something symbolic.

'Do you remember The Alamo?'

Simone and Luc exchanged bemused glances.

'Well that's all you need to do.'

He moved to the third step of the staircase. And from his superior position, in a voice designed to inform and inspire, addressed them. 'The Battle of the Alamo took place in 1836. Mexican troops brutally killed all but two of the brave Texan fighters defending the Alamo mission. That defeat spurred many Texans and US troops into joining the Texan army who then took revenge on the Mexicans by defeating them royally at The Battle of San Jacinto later the same year. A situation very like our own. We will not be defeated. We will stand strong and defend what is ours. So remember The Alamo; remember 1836.'

He seemed quite delighted with himself, incorporating flamboyant arm movements to illustrate his account of the historical event. Slaying imaginary fighters, marching to inaudible drums, holding aloft the Texan flag.

'Ok Dad. Great idea. Remember the Alamo it is.' Behind his father's back, Luc grinned, and used his right index finger to point repeatedly to his right temple in another well-known symbolic act.

Simone did not move a muscle throughout Alan's rant. She was feeling increasingly anxious, an overwhelming sense of foreboding flowing through her veins. This ranting madman was unrecognisable as her lovely Alain. Where has that man gone – the one she married? And now, she realises she doesn't have a clue what to do to get him *back.*

Annual review

May 2012

Alan didn't know what to expect. It had been some weeks – even months – since he'd seen Hugh. Another thing slipping as he struggled to keep up with the relentless demand at work. Good intentions ending up in the recycle bin in a never ending circle of missed opportunities and further resolve.

They met at their old haunt Café Royal on the corner of Rose Street. The framed rugby jerseys sat better with them than the chrome and faux leather of the former pubs, once The Drovers and now *Rouge!*, once The White Heather and now reincarnated as a hugely incongruous *Fiesta.*

Hugh, taking delivery of a large plate of mussels, was leaning in to whisper some doubtless risqué comment to the black-aproned waitress. He waved Alan over to the corner table, flashing one final conspiratorial smile at the server as he stood up to shake his friend's hand.

'Sit down, sit down. What kept you? Don't tell me. *I've got a pain Doctor. I've had it for week.'* He mimed an old hunched figure clutching his right side. *'Could it be appendicitis Doctor?'*

'Nothing that out of the ordinary, Hugh. Just the usual snuffles and sore throats, followed by a pile of paperwork. It will all end one day – just not any time soon unfortunately. Anyway, how are you?'

'Oh grand, grand. Well, I mean not brilliant of course, but coping, coping I'd say. Hard to believe but it's well over a year now as you know.'

Alan shook his head as if to ponder the relentless passage of time.

'Let me get you a pint – what's it to be?'

Alan sat down in the slightly battered leather armchair, sighing, removing his coat and scarf slowly as if using his last few breaths. He watched Hugh walking over to the bar, noting his slight stoop and more noticeably diminished frame.

'Are you well Hugh? Are you eating? How are you sleeping?'

'Christ, man. You're not in the surgery now. I'm fine. Another year older. Aren't we all? But given events of the past year, I wouldn't show up on any scale you might try to use on me, as anything other than *'as expected. Nothing to report.'*

They passed the next few minutes batting the conversational ball back and forwards in a comfortable exchange of the day to day details of life in the middle aged arena.

In an attempt to hold the centre court, Hugh began to relay a set of departmental anecdotes.

'And Jenny, you know that tidy out-patient nurse I've mentioned in the past? – Well she came in to the staff kitchen with an ice cube tray. Don't anyone put this in their diet coke by the way, she shouted. It's a urine sample!'

'And then Mrs Grey and Dumpy from Niddrie, when asked if she had any problems with her sex life, said *"would you stop giving Willie these wee blue peels doacter. I was just getting used to havin' Sunday afternoons to maself. And now he's started botherin' me again. I'm fair seek o' it."'*

Alan smiled wanly but didn't add any from his own fund of stories.

Once he'd realised that his attempts at levity were not bearing fruit, Hugh changed tack. 'You're not your usual self tonight Alan. What's eating you?'

'Och, just a bit weary that's all. A rest. That's what I need. All right for you. You had two months off. I could do with that.'

And then, realising what he'd said. 'Geez, Hugh. I'm sorry. That was a stupid, insensitive thing to say. Whatever ails me, it doesn't compare to losing your wife. I'm losing the plot here.'

Hugh waved away his apology.

'Talking of wives – how is the lovely Simone? I haven't seen her since that day at the cemetery. We both had a bit of a bubble at the grave, thinking of Anne being gone for a whole year.'

Alan had to rack his brains – that day at the grave? Recently? He could swear she hadn't told him about that. He thought out loud, 'sometimes I wonder what she gets up to when I'm out all day.'

'Well, you should be relieved she can make her own life and not be pestering you, like some of these doctors' wives. Always needing attention. Always organising social events and dragging you along. Or worse still, demanding ever bigger cars and designer handbags. You just need to keep her happy between the sheets old boy.'

Given the look on Alan's face it was then Hugh's turn to wish he'd thought before speaking.

'Em, that's not still a problem is it Alan? We can get you some help if it is.'

'Oh yes, and I'll be the next character you'll be mentioning in your funny stories. French wife of local GP asks for wee blue pills but wonders if she can have them in pink to match the bedroom. Nah, it's not that. I just wonder if I can trust her, that's all. Middle aged, Mediterranean, menopausal, needing to know she's still attractive. And all day to worry about it.'

'Look here Alan. It's one thing having theories about what women of a certain age worry about and then adding in the fact that she's French, as if that somehow makes her more likely to stray, but with no evidence to support your theory, that's all it is. A theory.

'Look at Finlay. I wondered for years if he was gay. Just a theory. A young, attractive, fit guy with no mention ever of a girlfriend. That didn't mean he was gay. He might have had loads of girls but didn't choose to bring them home. He might have had a relationship with a married woman which had to be kept secret. He might even have had a steady girlfriend in Africa who was black. Most likely the girl wasn't suitable in some way for genteel Glasgow society and he didn't want to upset the old parents.'

'So – is he gay?' Alan was intrigued now.

'Well, as it happens he's bisexual. He's only just opened up about it. And only to me. That's almost worse than being gay in the old folks' eyes. He gets plenty of scope out in Africa.'

'So what are trying to say Hugh? Your theory was almost correct?'

'No. It remained a theory until I had some confirmatory evidence, which Finlay happened to present me with.'

'And don't you mind?'

'What – that he's bisexual? Or that he didn't tell me?'

'Either – both.'

'No, not really. I wouldn't have done anything differently if I'd known years ago. And it saved me letting the cat out of the bag I suppose. I'm just making the point that it's easy to put two and two together and get the proverbial five. Now, you'd better order some food and put some lead in your pencil.'

'Very funny, Hugh. And here I was, wondering how you were coping on your own. And ready to offer some sympathy and support. And all I get is a lecture on research principles. I should have known better. Order me a beef and ale pie would you? I'm off to the gents. Watching out for bisexuals on the way.'

Alan left the pub satisfied that Hugh was coping with his widowed state, and had even recovered some of his usual joie de vivre. As he drove home through the streets of East Edinburgh, the streetlights pooling their yellow gleam on the rain soaked surfaces, he mulled over their discussion, thinking again about theories and evidence, diagnosis and proof.

Finlay bisexual. That was a bit of surprise. Finlay had always been just Hugh's little brother, an occasional visitor to Edinburgh, and when in conversation, the topic was inevitably his work in Africa rather than his private life. He'd been a peripheral character, heard about rather than seen around, a generation younger, it felt, from Hugh and Alan, living a very different and remote life.

And yet – he'd had quite an influence on Luc over the years. Encouraging the boy in his artwork, suggesting gap year opportunities, engineering some work experience in that youth project in Glasgow.

Maybe the lad was around more than Alan had at first recalled.

1992 or 93? Alan wasn't sure exactly when, but Luc must have been about 3 or 4. It was in France, The Vendée. A hot sunny afternoon. Finlay was playing with all the children at the tideline whilst the four adults lay comatose on their beach mats out of sight in the dunes. Luc comes running as fast as his little legs will carry him, crying 'Papa, Papa, they've buried Uncle Finlay and they're laughing and I think he might be dead! Come and save him quick, quick!' He'd attached himself like a limpet to Finlay, for the rest of the holiday.

Eight or nine years later? Kenmore. Finlay and Luc went boating on the loch with a picnic and a plan to land on the small island to go exploring. Luc said 'We had the best time ever Papa, I do love Uncle Finlay. I wish he lived with us.'

And that summer after he left school, Luc pleading with him, 'Please let me go Dad; you said you didn't want me wasting the summer hanging around the park. I can be doing some good if I go to work with Finlay.'

Christ!

And only this summer, Finlay, Luc and Andrew in their matching headbands, tents under arms, driving off to T in the Park.

'My God. All those opportunities and more. How could we have been so trusting?'

By the time Alan reached home he could hardly release his hands from the wheel, he'd been gripping it so hard.

'If he's laid a hand on my boy, I'll murder him.'

Please tell your doctor

The same evening

'Don't tell me NO-ONE suspected anything!' Alan bellowed at her. 'SOMEONE must have seen or heard SOMETHING in all that time to make them suspicious!'

He paced back and forth between the table and the window, his legs making quick, firm, movements, his arms waving erratically. So wound-up that Simone could feel waves of anger emanating from him, even though she was sitting at the other end of the room. It was the nearest place to an exit she could get. With each turn that he made from table to window or from window to table, she grew increasingly nervous.

She tried to look blank.

'All these years – ALL these years he's been allowed to play with the children. Taking them off on his own to out of the way places for God's sake.

Anything could have happened! ANYTHING! And WE let him do it. We're very lucky that Luc hasn't been buggered Simone. BUGGERED! Do you hear me?

'Alain, please, will you calm down. You're making Finlay sound like a paedophile when he's not.'

She instantly regretted her response when Alan stopped pacing and turned on her furiously, shouting, 'I want to tear his fucking head off Simone. Tear it right OFF! And how do you know he's not, Simone, eh? How would YOU know where Finlay has and hasn't been, or what he has and hasn't done?'

She started to shake then and clasped her arms around her shoulders in a vain attempt to keep herself still, as the old holiday memory came flooding back and she knew she had a decision to make and to make it quickly. What *was* she going to say to Alan, who was now standing right in front of her, looking redder and angrier than she'd ever seen him in all their married life.

She had gone wandering off after the big lunch at the Loch Tay Inn, looking for somewhere peaceful to have a cigarette when she'd seen him, standing at the loch's edge, staring out over the water into the distance.

'Finlay, may I join you? Or do you prefer to be alone?'

He had turned and smiled politely. 'No. Yeah, feel free.'

She had pulled out a cigarette and offered him one.

'No thanks. I've given up. Please don't tempt me.'

They had stood there in companionable silence for a while, gazing at the scenery.

'Beautiful, isn't it?' he'd eventually remarked. 'One of Scotland's finest.'

'Yes,' she'd replied, looking sideways at him, intently. 'But I believe that you are also thinking about something else beautiful that is a long way from here, maybe?'

He hadn't answered, only given her a tired smile, the lines deep around his eyes, a legacy of too much sun.

She'd tried to be clever, wanting to test out her theory, thinking that now was a good time. 'You can't fool old Simone you know. You may be here but your heart is in Africa, isn't it? With a certain someone, I think?'

He turned to face her, and with his eyes wide, his brows lifting, he reminded her of an overgrown schoolboy. 'And if it was . . .?'

She had felt her excitement mounting then, and had moved in with a pincer-like response. 'And if it is . . . then I am glad for you. About time, is it not, that Finlay came under a lover's spell?'

He shook his head, turned to her with eyes downcast, 'Simone. Don't pry any further. You have no idea what you're talking about.'

She had pulled a face, pretended to be affronted. 'Finlay! I am French! If anyone is an expert in matters of the heart it is the French – the whole world knows that! I can just tell with you, you can't hide it from me. You have the look, the demeanour of a man who has fallen. So what can be the problem with that?'

He returned another weary smile, the creases by his eyes appearing even deeper.

'Simone my friend, I couldn't even begin to explain.'

And she had known then, guessed the truth of it, and hadn't been able to resist pushing him the last step of the way.

'Well don't then! I'm sure that you and he will work it out if it's meant to be.' Then she had turned away, intending to walk back to the hotel alone. But he had been totally shocked, and had grabbed her arm so firmly she'd had to stop. 'Wait! Don't just walk off like that. What did you say again?'

She repeated herself calmly, putting a little extra emphasis on the 'you and *he*'.

At that he had let her arm go and shrugged his shoulders, his lungs letting out a rush of air. 'How did you guess?'

'Don't worry,' she had said in a soothing voice. 'You haven't done anything, not given anything away. It's just, well, my intuition is highly developed, that's all. I will keep it to myself, your little secret. It's safe with me. You have my word.'

He had been rubbing his forehead and eyebrows all the while she'd been talking. Then he had breathed deeply and smoothed his brows down into tidy arches again with his long, tanned fingers before answering.

'I don't want the family to know, Simone. Don't get me wrong – I'm not ashamed of myself – and there have been women too, you'll be pleased to know. But Hugh, Anne in particular – would never understand, and the perceived shame would kill my parents – God knows my relationship with them is fragile enough as it is.'

She had reassured him again. 'Why should they know if you don't want to tell them, Finlay? You live in Africa. What you do there is your own business. But be careful, eh? The family would not like to lose you, I say. You are very precious to them, even if you don't always realise it.'

His face had lifted, so that he had looked a little younger. 'Yeah, you're probably right. Thanks. Thanks, Simone.'

Noisy shouting had alerted them to the children

running across the field, calling for him, so she had wandered off for another cigarette, wearing a triumphant grin, feeling very pleased with herself for being so clever at wheedling secrets out of people.

Simone looked up and faced her husband.

'WELL?' he yelled. 'I'll ask you again Simone. How would you know about Finlay? Or . . .'

He can see her guilty face, she knows it.

'WHAT do you know about Finlay's past?'

Simone looked up and faced her husband.

'Well?' he yelled. 'I'll ask you again Simone. Did YOU already know Finlay was a fucking poof?'

She is caught like an animal in the glare of a car's headlights, not knowing which way to run to avoid danger. Shall she come clean or lie? He is burning with anger. She decides on truth, and takes a deep breath.

'Yes, Alain, I knew.'

'Jesus, Simone – and you didn't tell me! When exactly DID you find out? Had Hugh already told you before he told me?'

'No Alain. Hugh has not said anything to me. I just guessed it.'

He is staring at her; she feels his eyes boring into her very soul.

'You just . . . guessed it. Interesting. When did you "just guess it"?'

'A long time ago. Maybe ten years or more. I knew when we were at Kenmore that first time. Finlay and I were outside smoking, sharing a few thoughts on life, that's all. I felt he was troubled.' She pauses, rubs her hands up and down her arms.

Alain is listening intently, for something more tangible than this. Her answer isn't good enough.

'Did HE tell you outright?'

She looks at her feet and says firmly, 'No. I asked him myself, because my intuition was saying something wasn't right. He never reacted to me in the way most men do, so I guessed he was gay.'

Alan turned the corner of his mouth up and lowered his voice. 'How do most men react to you Simone?'

'Alain, don't be silly. You know the answer to that question. They look at me in 'that' way. I am a woman – I used to be a very attractive woman – most men react to that.'

'Most men – so you mean young men? Old men? *Any* man?' He almost spits out the words.

She has said too much and attempts to bring the focus back to Finlay. 'Alain, don't look for more trouble. I am generalising. And you're wrong about Finlay. He is not gay, he's bisexual. And I think his sex life is none of our business. Please calm down.

He's not a paedophile and never will be. He's a decent honest man doing a valuable job overseas. The very reason he's never come out and told people is precisely because he fears the kind of reaction you are showing. It's unreasonable.'

Alan shuts his eyes and shakes his head vigorously from side to side. His colour no less heightened.

'I can't believe you are calling me unreasonable. I can't believe you have known about Finlay for ten years and never been considerate enough to tell me, so I could have made a decision about the safety of OUR child. I can't believe that my own wife has kept this knowledge a secret. What other secrets do you have Simone? When am I going to find out the truth about other things from someone else eh?'

She shivers and summons up some energy to reply. 'This isn't fair Alain. Why must you always find something to argue about these days? You never used to be like a bear with a sore head all the time, so angry, so unhappy. *Please* go see a doctor and get some help. I beg you.'

His eyes are shut, his mind closed to her plea. When he opens them he won't look at her, instead he stares over the top of her head at the blank wall behind. 'And which caring, sharing doctor would that be then, Simone? One of the disillusioned, uncaring partners in my practice? My 'best friend' Hugh who has also kept this secret from me for years, or one of his money-making cronies in the hallowed halls of the Infirmary? I wouldn't give ANY of them the time of day. It's called 'Hobson's Choice' Simone. Look it up if you haven't heard of it.'

When the door slams she rises stiffly and makes her way to the kitchen. Cooking brandy will do for now. It will warm her up her body at least. But it won't reach her heart. She thinks it is better not to look into that, pretend it is still whole, and that another piece has not died.

A serious complaint

A few weeks later

Isobel was surprised, delighted and almost unbelieving to find herself at a partners' meeting in mid-August, to present the annual review of patient complaints – the doctors having responded to her very first request to set a date. Her usual repertoire of techniques – ask nicely, remind, remind again, foretell dire consequences of failure, demand, rant and rave and finally threaten to resign, had somehow not been necessary this year. Tom Windsor was on annual leave or she might have believed that pigs indeed could fly.

'Now I've already sent you my draft report,' she started. But then with a sigh and a barely perceptible shake of the head she continued, 'however, just in case you've forgotten to bring it with you, here's a copy for each of you.'

With a slight cough and a wink to Alan, George

Dailly responded, 'best if you take us through it, Isobel. It's some time since I read it and I'd appreciate a look at the detail as well as hearing your overview.'

'Well, facts and figures first then. Over the year 25 complaints. Ten more than last year where we averaged one a month. Five of them about admin issues – staff sent the prescription to the wrong pharmacy, Mrs Jones invited for a flu vaccine *yet again* when she tells us every year she believes it *gives* you flu, Mr Black didn't like how he was spoken to by 'that Glaswegian' we have on reception (uppity cow apparently), Major Reid will not under any circumstances be asked *what is the problem* when he wants an urgent appointment, and old Mrs Grant's daughter can't see why we won't make an appointment available for her with the nurse to fit in with the Tuesday club. Just the usual stuff around expectations, procedures, human error. And all sorted in-house thankfully.'

'Yes, you do a good job Isobel. Fortunately you can deal with these issues without involving us. Now what about the other 20?'

'Well there was the usual miscellany – icy paths despite what Mr O'Brien pays 'the bastard council' every year to clear them. Excuse my French. And then the lack of appointments. We'll never get round that one if I live to be a 100. Oh and why does it take so long to get an insurance report completed? Again, I usually find some empathetic listening, followed by an insight into the workings of the appointment system or the GP contract, coupled with an agreed action of some type satisfies the complainant.'

Alan checked his watch. Six o'clock.

'Is this discussion going anywhere? Or are we just rubber-stamping your report Isobel? In which case can I say that I have the utmost respect for how you handle some of these awkward buggers, and I'm 100 per cent confident your report will meet the usual Health Board criteria of *lessons learned and subsequent appropriate action plan for the coming year*. Now can I go home and have something to eat and a large whisky? It's Friday night and I'm beat.'

Isobel looked to George.

'It's the remaining 15 complaints we're more concerned about Alan,' said George. 'And we all need to be here to discuss them. I assume you haven't looked at the report in any detail?

Without waiting for a response, George turned back to Isobel, 'I think I'm right in assuming that the other 15 complaints concern us doctors. Right Isobel?' She nodded.

'And how does that compare with last year?'

'Three times as many.'

Helen interjected, 'and was last year different from previous years in that respect?'

'No. We usually get five or six a year. Have done for years now.'

George took back the baton. 'And what do you put the increase down to, Isobel?'

'Em. Well. How can I put this? It appears that a number of patients don't like your attitude.'

'Is that *my* attitude, or are you referring to all of us doctors? And are you including Susan in this?'

'No, Dr Dailly, not Susan. The only thing that happened with her was that she forgot to refer that child to Audiology, you remember. We sorted that out, made a significant event of it, and I'm sure that was a one-off.'

'Well, spit out then. Or is it just that we're all grumpy, irritable sods who run late, don't listen and hurry patients out of the door?'

'Well, it's not just that simple.' Isobel breathed in audibly. 'Over the year there were two complaints each about you, Dr Windsor and Dr King. And the other nine concerned Dr Fraser.'

She looked at the floor. 'I'm sorry Dr Fraser.'

'Nothing to be sorry about woman. Just a freak year. Don't you understand statistics? This year is just an outlier. On its own it means nothing. Anyway, we all know patients are getting more demanding – and you two do your best to leave me with all the heart-sinks. Do you think I don't notice? Do you think I'm buttoned up the back? I bet they're the ones who complain. Isn't that correct Isobel?'

'Not exactly. In fact, hardly at all. Look, what I've

done is, I've drawn up a table with the names and the key points of their complaints – just for the purposes of discussion. That detail doesn't go in the report. And by the way, they're all sorted, these complaints. You don't need to worry about that. But we need to say what we've learned and what action we'll take.'

She handed out a copy to each of the three partners.

'Look Isobel, how about you leave this with us? I promise we'll come back to you with what you need to complete the report. You get off home now. We'll lock up.' George stood up and moved to show her out of the staffroom.

Alan continued to read the information. Then he pushed his chair back angrily and stood up.

'What is this? A fucking witch-hunt or something? Christ. Just write the usual claptrap and send it off. Copy last year's and change the dates. Who the fuck even reads these reports? It's just another tick-box exercise.'

'Alan. Sit down. We will sort the report and keep it suitably bland and general. There'll be no names and we can explain away the increase using some jargon or other. As long as we show willingness to take action that keeps them happy. And I know for a fact that down the road they get a lot more complaints than we do – especially about lack of appointments. So I doubt if anything will come back from this.'

'Good. Surely we can all go home now. You can give Isobel what she needs.' Alan checked his watch again, before refolding his cuffs to equalise the depth on both sleeves and reaching for his jacket.

George looked at Helen. Then turned back to Alan.

'Truth is Alan – we're worried about you. The complaints tell only part of the story – *angry, impatient, fails to listen, dismissive.* I've got another list from staff. Do you want to hear that?'

'Now you're having me on. Demanding difficult patients are one thing. But I've always had a good relationship with staff. Come on. You know that.'

Alan looked for reassurance to Helen. 'Helen. Back me up here.'

She looked away.

George continued in as neutral a voice as he could muster. 'Alan – you **did** have a good relationship with staff. For all the many years you've been here. Until the last year or two. And it's only because you did that we've held back on this. But it seems something's changed. I'm hearing *volatile, moody, fit to explode, harsh with mistakes, irritable beyond belief.* ' Apparently it's a relief to all when you're on annual leave.'

'Give me names George! Yeh, give me names! I'll go straight to whoever it is and sort this out once and for all.'

'Alan. Stop it. Calm down. Look at yourself. You're

purple in the face. You're shaking. What is it all about?'

'I'm going home. You'd better all take a look at yourselves before you start on me. This is ridiculous nonsense and I won't listen to it. Everywhere you go these days someone is judging you. Audits, appraisals, reviews, and bloody revalidation soon. Let me be a fucking doctor. Let me do what I was trained to do. Annual review of complaints? I'm away to write my own. And I won't spare my so-called partners. I'm disgusted with the pair of you.'

There were three doors between the staff room and the car park. He slammed every one.

'Well that didn't go too well, did it?' sighed George, after the third slam.

'Phew. I suppose when you think about it George, we're telling him he's impatient, grumpy, volatile and so on. Why did we think he'd ever sit and discuss all this rationally?' Helen squirmed uncomfortably in her chair.

George put his hand to his temple and rubbed it up and down slowly. 'We'll need to go for the extra-ordinary partners' meeting then. Unless you've got any other bright ideas. Thank God we finally managed to draw up that partnership agreement or we'd have been on a sticky wicket. Do you want to spend time now planning a strategy or will we come back to it later when Tom's back? But it'll have to be soon. This can't go on.'

'I agree.' Helen nodded. 'It cannot. Let's decide now what we think should be the outcome and then we can draft up an agenda to achieve that. And I'll check the terms of the partnership agreement for how soon we can call the meeting and anything else relevant about procedures. Is that okay?'

George blew out through his rather fleshy lips and shook his head sadly. 'I've known the guy for years. I hate to see this happening to him. But there's no doubt in my mind, he's heading for meltdown. Now what are we thinking here? Sabbatical maybe? Let's go for a drink and think about where we go from here shall we?'

Armed with a gin and tonic, George and Helen went over again what they had agreed. They had to act in the best interests of the practice – no question about that.

'I'm really concerned that Alan has been under too much pressure of late. We should have approached him earlier to see if we could help'

'Rather you than me Helen. I'm not sure how he would have taken that. Although it would have looked better than just springing this on him.

'I'd like to see him recover his usual equanimity.

There is definitely no question of a split, agreed? We should think about suggesting that he takes some time off to have a rest and then a change of scene.'

'We could all do with that, and next year maybe you could do the same George. Don't take that the wrong way though!'

'Maybe Alan could go to his beloved France and do a bit of research. Or perhaps he could arrange an exchange with one of the island GPs needing an injection of capital city life. But he must have a break, definitely that.'

'But then there'll be the question of who would cover. Susan could maybe do an extra day as a retainer. That's allowed and would defray part of the cost. Do you think you could sound her out Helen? Alan could get himself signed off as burnt out – unlikely he'd agree to that. But the insurance would at least pay for a locum for the other days.'

George didn't sleep well that night. He recounted the details of his dream to his wife the next morning. Patients were queued at his nightmare surgery door, all the way out of the building and down the street. Isobel had gone white-haired overnight. Helen was simultaneously performing a rectal examination on one patient and an eye test on another. Tom was injecting whisky into his arm and Alan was walking the streets wearing a sandwich board which read 'Jobless! My GP partners failed to care!'

Alan threw the typewritten letter across the dinner table to Simone.

'Take a look at that. Bastards. Scheming bastards!'

'What, what. What is it Alain?'

'Those partners of mine want an extra-ordinary partners' meeting. And there is only one item on the agenda. Arrangements for the coming year. I know what that's about. They want me out. Christ would you believe it?'

Dr Alexander Sneddon, who is also the current president of the Scottish Institute for Rural Health, believes sabbaticals for GPs will help to invigorate the profession and help prevent burnout without impacting on GP numbers in Scotland.

That's what his 'caring', 'sharing' practice partners had told Alan. But he wasn't fooled by the official line reeled out to back up the words carefully spoken by George Dailly.

'We all agree it's the best thing for everyone at this time Alan. The best option for you and the best option for the practice too. We're sure you'll enjoy being able to focus exclusively on your research project and that you'll bring some kudos back here with you as a result by the time you return next year.'

Alan was furious. It was all soft soap, just lots of lather to cover up their embarrassment at asking him to take time-out, before he totally burnt-out. It was insulting, ridiculously judgemental, yet there wasn't a damn thing he could do about it since a majority decision had been made under the rules of the partnership agreement. A decision that he believed had been made well in advance of the confrontational practice meeting where they had called his bluff. The scheming, untrustworthy bastards. Every last damn one of them. After all he'd done for the patients *and* the practice for *all* these years. He was no angel to work with, he knew that. He agreed he was tired, and he could be grouchy at times, but who wouldn't be with his workload and mounting problems at home? They'd blown it up out of all proportion. Read meanings into things he'd supposedly said that he'd never intended. Focused on the couple of patient complaints made against him and not the many plaudits. He'd felt completely under attack during the meeting.

They hadn't wanted to listen to anything he'd tried to say in his defence.

He'd eventually stormed out, slamming the surgery door behind him, and had only gone back after hours to pick up his files, top up the supplies in his medical bag and fetch the University's portable computer containing all his project information. The next two weeks he entered and left the surgery without engaging with anyone other than patients, completing all his reports and leaving a clear desk.

He'd now been home for a whole week, and wasn't at all sure what he'd achieved since then, other than informing the University that he'd be leaving for Paris shortly to assist with the setting up of the French component of the multi-region research project. But in truth, he had no appetite for it at present. He was still too angry, too distracted. Thoughts buzzed in his head like bees around a beekeeper, and they would not be stilled. He hadn't slept a night through this week yet because of his whirling brain, and other than doping himself up (no – he would not give in to *that* just yet) or a good orgasm (hardly likely with his current pathetic performances) or going to see a doctor (*no* bloody chance), he didn't know how to improve matters.

Compound Fracture

October 2012

Simone had not been the understanding, consoling wife he'd expected. Only the day before yesterday, he'd suggested they walk together along their favourite stretch of the beach but she had brushed off his approach with a dismissive 'I need to be alone, Alain. I need to think.'

Yesterday, dressed city smart, she left with barely a word. 'I'm going to meet a client.'

'You didn't mention that yesterday. Seems you don't share much with me these days.'

'Alain, you're not normally here. I'm just doing what I always do. I'm going to meet Andrea from Jenners for a couple of hours and then I'll be home.'

With nothing better to do, he decided to start packing his suitcase even though he wasn't due to leave for another two weeks. But first the list. In his carry-on bag he'd put his binoculars, laptop, passport, Euros and tickets as well as his MP3 player and headphones to facilitate any necessary escape from conversation on the plane.

Into the suitcase went his pyjamas, silk dressing gown, several pairs of unopened socks, his moleskin trousers, brown brogues, his Aran jumper, assorted checked shirts. He planned to lay his navy suit on top of the other clothes and in preparation, would hang it up in view. When he went to the spare room closet where it usually hung, sandwiched between Simone's summer jackets, it wasn't there.

Where is it? She knows that's where I keep that suit. I always hang it there. She's so disorganised she drives me mad.

He couldn't possibly wait till she got home. He dialled her number, hoping that she'd actually answer it.

'Alain. What is it? I'm busy here.'

'Simone, where the heck is my navy suit? You haven't sent it to the cleaners have you? I'll need it for France.'

'Yes, I have, but what's the rush? You're not going for another two weeks.'

'Just tell me where the ticket is and I'll go and pick it up now.'

Alan heard what sounded like a man's whisper – 'White or Red Simone?'

'Give me a minute Alain.'

Then she answered 'Red please, Jack.'

'The ticket's on the noticeboard in the kitchen. You'll find it. Bye.'

Eventually he found the ticket next amidst an assortment of notices, old and long out of date. Flyers, pamphlets, cuttings.

He'd have a quick cup of coffee before braving the High Street.

Before he'd drunk even half of it, the question 'Red or White?' popped into his mind. She must have been having wine. And then, who the hell is Jack?

'I picked up my suit,' he said to Simone as she walked through the door.

'Oh good,' she replied, hanging her coat over the back of the chair.

'Enjoy your lunch?'

'Yes, very nice actually.'

'And did Jack enjoy his?'

'Yes. Why are you asking such a silly question?'

'Because you said you were going to lunch with Andrea. So there must be something else you're not telling me.'

'I was supposed to have lunch with Andrea. Jenners sent Jack instead.'

'Oh really?'

'Yes, really. You're acting as though you don't believe me?'

'Actually, I'm not sure I do.'

'You are becoming unreasonable. I feel like I'm walking on eggshells around you. I'm getting tired. My sleep is disturbed by all this nonsense. I'm feeling unwell. I can't stand you being around the house all day, under my feet, prodding things, moving objects around, checking for dust everywhere!'

'For God's sake Simone I'm *not* checking for dust!' he'd shouted at her after her onslaught of complaints. 'I've got better things to do with my time than that.'

'Yes you are! You are! You're doing nothing useful with your time at all; you're driving me crazy!' She'd screamed back, before running out to her studio and bolting the door behind her.

The next morning she got up early, left him a note to say she was going out shopping for the day with a friend. He read it, scrunched it up and threw it into the fireplace. Now he's sitting at the dining table staring out of the window, his left hand in a fist, pressing against his lips, holding his anger in, the fingers of his right hand drumming the table in quick, small pulses which are building up to a crescendo and then a sudden *slam* of an open palm onto the table top. He jumps up from his chair too quickly, almost overbalancing, and the chair scrapes backwards as he does so. The noise is enough to cause him to slow a little, check his movement and decide exactly where to start his search.

He'd once heard a female lecturer from the University say that the first thing she'd done on sabbatical leave was to clean out her cupboards. She'd told him that the act of clearing, sorting and cleaning had been 'cathartic' in both a physical sense and a psychological sense. She had quite literally cleared the decks and then she'd been able to concentrate fully on her research for the rest of the leave period. Well then, if Simone asks, that's exactly what he's doing. It would be a good cover for his real motives, which will need to be hidden from her until he has enough evidence to confront her. There has to be something, somewhere, and he's damn well going to find it. It's obvious – she *has* to be hiding the truth from him.

When Simone returns, she calls Alan's name, but doesn't get an answer, so begins looking for him. She's shocked to find him sitting on the dining room floor surrounded by the entire contents of their large chest of drawers, except for the top drawer containing the cutlery and place mats. There are about a hundred photographs on his left, placed in a huge arc, like a deck of cards fanned out by a magician. Some of these have post-its placed on them; red ones, yellow ones and green ones, not in any apparent order, yet there's some writing on the yellow ones.

Behind him, the sewing box has been emptied out and its buttons are in piles, colour coded. The three pairs of scissors it contained have been lined up on the floor in order of size. The bits and bobs box is also behind him, intact, but with a post-it on top which states 'TBD'.

To his right are several piles of old maps, guide books, pamphlets, postcards and general ephemera. Also a few boxes of jigsaw puzzles. He is holding a map of France between his outstretched arms, looking at it studiously.

Simone can't believe the sight. 'My God Alain! This is a terrible mess! What the hell are you doing?'

He looks up from the map slowly and meets her flashing eyes. His speech is measured. 'It's not a mess Simone. I'm simply sorting out decades of accumulated junk which no one has bothered to do before now. I'd appreciate it if you do not touch anything here until I have finished – which is not going to be by tonight, given the magnitude of the task.'

'Don't worry Alain,' she replies, 'It's all yours. Looks like I have a dinner to prepare since you've not done that. Perhaps you can tell me where we are going to eat it however, because there is no longer room in here to sit up to the table.'

As she turns and leaves, he drops his head to look at the map of the Vendée again. There is something niggling him, a significant place name that conjures up an uneasy feeling, rather than a solid memory. He's hoping that if he keeps concentrating he may retrieve the memory to go with it.

When he wakes at 3.30am, after a few hours of his subconscious at work, it has indeed surfaced. He was cooking coq au vin in the gite where they'd stayed that year, and serving it up to everyone, whilst Hugh filled the wine glasses, and they all got slowly drunk. There are quite a few photos of them there that he found earlier, (and put them into the 'holidays' classification using yellow post-its), raising glasses to *La France, old friends, le vin.* Pictures of Hugh and Anne, himself and Simone, Anne and Simone, Hugh and Simone. But not one of himself and Anne. Why ever not? He remembered making love with Simone that very night. She'd jumped all over him as soon as they'd gone to bed, insistent that such a perfect evening must be consummated. He'd managed, just about, and then they'd fallen into a deep stupor. The next day she'd been unable to get up so he'd left her in bed and gone with Anne and Hugh and the kids to the theme park where he had taken more holiday photos.

The memory comes faster now, and he can see it clearly as if it's a film on a TV screen.

He'd watched her at supper, moving lithely between the kitchen and table outside, her white dress floating in folds around her knees, the v-shaped neckline showing off her ample cleavage. She'd looked gorgeous, and all the better for a day in bed getting rid of her migraine. Yet despite his persistent advances she'd not been interested in sex that night, saying she was still tired. He'd felt peeved, given he'd been running around after children all day, whilst she'd been resting, but hadn't made a fuss about it, not wanting to fall out during the holiday, even though he'd had to wait two more days before she was willing again.

The photograph sorting continues the next day. Alan pulls out every one related to a holiday, and then sub-divides these into different holidays, arranging them chronologically. Yes, here are the ones of the Vendée again that he found yesterday, and a few new photos too. These are of the theme park trip they made. Luc with Emily, Andrew and Anne waving back at the camera. Himself with the three children standing next to the rocket. No Hugh. There are none of Hugh.

Alan's head suddenly hurts. His brainwaves spike as he remembers that it's because Hugh wasn't there. Of course. Hugh had been suffering a terrible hangover and remained behind with only Simone in the gite. All day. Just the two of them. Could they have? Would they have?

He quickly picks up the rest of the Vendée photos and carries them over to the table, pushing the other things to one side. He homes in on the picture of Simone in her white dress. She is sitting at the table next to Hugh, on the opposite side to Anne. The three of them have been engaged in animated banter, just old friends enjoying each other's company. Alan's eyes drill down to Simone. She is laughing, holding a wine glass in her right hand, looking sideways on to the camera, but her left arm is very close to Hugh's right. Alan snatches the photo off the dining table and jogs upstairs with it to his study. He turns on the computer, places the photo under the printer cover and makes a scan. When he blows up the image, although it's pixelated and a bit grainy, he can see – he really can see it now – Simone's and Hugh's legs are touching underneath the table.

His heart quickens. They could have.

Significant? Yes. But on its own, it's not enough. As a clinician he's well aware that he needs incontrovertible proof to draw absolute conclusions – and he doesn't have it, not yet. But what he does have is time on his side. A whole 50 weeks of it. And he will be careful, methodical, clinical, cover all eventualities and everyone's tracks. He doesn't even need their cooperation and neither can they stop him. He'll tell no one what he's doing because no one can be trusted.

He makes a list.

Chest of drawers – check first.

Cupboards and wardrobes – search next.

Luc's room – be careful.

Simone's studio – be *very* careful.

The chest of drawers yielded nothing, unless you count a sexy set of purple lingerie he's never seen Simone wear.

The cupboards and wardrobes were crammed full of clothes and shoes. They'd need a half day's sorting out at least to see if everything still fitted and looked good or not. That could wait.

The forbidden ground of Luc's room was a revelation. The disorganised and messy adolescent boy's space of a few years ago showed a significant improvement, with several attempts at classifying and reordering possessions. Gone were the piles of dirty underwear on the mat, empty coke cans, and plates of snack-food left-overs that Alan had abhorred. Instead there were files of drawings, labelled by subject. A CD collection stacked in two stands, in alphabetical order of artist. Tasteful (well, mostly) posters neatly arranged on the walls. There was hope for the boy yet.

The copy of 'Men Only' under the bed was a surprise, a pleasant surprise actually, given recent worries about gays and Finlay. Alan sat on the bed and flicked slowly through, pausing to admire the photographs. 'Nice . . . Mmm . . . I wouldn't mind getting lucky with that one . . . Now SHE'd help me get it up properly again!' The words 'You Dirty Old Man' came to mind. He shook his head and put the magazine back carefully into its original position.

So far one photo and a load of niggling memories, some hazy, some clearer, some uncomfortable, depending on his interpretation. Tomorrow he'd tackle Simone's studio – her inner sanctum. He made sure the key was in its usual place, and lifting it carefully off the hook, he ran his fingers over it, and then held it up before his eyes, screwing them tighter in an effort to focus his thoughts.

Could this be the key to open her box of secrets? She has to be keeping secrets from him, and where better to store them than in her studio, from which everyone is banned under pain of death? It's 4pm. There's not enough time today to start his quest, but what about tomorrow? Tomorrow Simone and Luc will be out all day and the one thing *he'll* have is time on his hands.

He replaces the key on the hook and turns to the fridge intending to take out some food for a quick snack. There's hardly enough in there to make even a cheese sandwich. She'll probably have forgotten to go shopping again today. He sighs in frustration. Nothing ever changes.

He puts plastic bags over his shoes and gloves on

his hands. Can't be too careful. He feels a certain frisson at turning the key in the lock, and snatches a quick glance behind him, just like a schoolboy squeezing through an orchard hedge to steal crab apples.

He closes the door gently after himself and locks it from the inside. Just in case. Casting his eyes about he's rather surprised to see that the room is not in the disorganised state he'd expected. In fact, it's pretty clean and tidy apart from the worktable which is strewn with plastic sheeting, empty cups, brushes, two small saucepans, some glue pots, an open packet of what looks like polyfilla, with white hardened blobs all around it, several tools which resemble instruments of torture, and a horribly realistic disembodied hand and wrist that grasps the edge of the table as if to stop itself falling off. He shudders; thinks, 'she's a bit weird, this wife of mine.'

The bookcase is very neat, with books running in order of height – small on the top shelf, to largest on the bottom. The big shelving unit (he remembers now the effort of putting that up for her years ago, and how she showed her gratitude afterwards) is stuffed full of models in various stages of completion, or for the ones covered in a thick layer of dust, abandonment.

He can't for the life of him see anything suspicious in any of this, so it's not worth risking picking it up in case he drops it, but why she would want to spend so much time here alone he still fails to comprehend.

The antique chest of drawers could store things out of sight, so he decides to search through that next, carefully – one drawer at a time. The first contains materials – offcuts, balls of wool, bits of tapestry, cotton reels. He can't see what all that has to do with sculpture, but what would he know? He moves on swiftly.

The second has a collection of tins. A large old biscuit tin containing a first aid kit. One with buttons in it. Another with tacks. The tins are so old they could be worth something, even if the contents are not, and nothing here is suspicious. He sighs with frustration and bends over to reach the next and last drawer.

It's stiff, he has to tug it a little to get it open, and tweaks his back in the process. There are untidy piles of ephemera relating to past exhibitions: posters, leaflets, tickets. He starts to lift the papers up, scanning his eyes quickly over them but finds nothing of interest.

Then his prying fingers find something square and hard beneath the posters rolled up in the bottom of the chest. He uses his free hand to move the posters to one side and the other to pick up the object. It's a CD case.

Cheltenham Jazz Festival 2006

Smokey Nights feat. Mack Robinson

Alan's eyes rove around the room searching for a CD player, but there isn't one that he can see anywhere, only a radio on the shelf above the sink, although there is a stack of CDs on top of one of the cupboards. He yanks open the door. The player is on the top shelf, a little dusty, clearly not having been in use for a while. He pulls it out and plugs it into the nearest socket, then continues moving around the room, opening cupboards and peering at their contents.

Hugh's voice starts up, loud, clear, and slightly husky. 'Smoothie,' Alan says out-loud, 'Typical.'

'Hi folks! It's great to see so many people here for our set. Let me introduce you to 'Smokey Nights', who've come all the way down from Bonnie Scotland to play just for you.'

The other band members are introduced in turn, followed by a round of applause for each. 'And last but definitely not least – myself on Bass – Hef Scott.'

More clapping and a 'Right on!'

'We're going to start off with three upbeat numbers you'll be sure to recognise, then we have a little surprise for you –you're going to love him I can guarantee. So – on with the show!'

'Take Five', 'Sunny' and 'It Had to be You' were played with energy and style. The audience seemed to be warming to the four guys from 'Bonnie Scotland' and applauded enthusiastically, with a few whoops thrown in.

Hugh's voice cuts in. 'Okay – thanks for that! We're just loving being here aren't we guys?'

'Hello Cheltenham!' Billy shouts.

'Hello Scotland!' a few voices shout back.

'And now – that surprise I mentioned. We're going to turn the lights down low and do a few ballads, and we have a great performer to sing them – please welcome the very cool, the very smooth, Mack Robinson!'

Christ – he really is hamming it up now, thinks Alan.

As the applause dies down, 'Love for Sale' starts, and Mack's deep voice sounds out after the band's first chord.

Alan listens intently, thinking he's making a passable job of it, but not as good as Tony Bennett's version.

He moves onto the five-drawer tool cabinet now, being careful not to touch any of the strange-looking instruments that occupy the drawers.

'And next, a very special song I'd like to dedicate to a certain Gypsy Girl I know. "You Do Something to Me". Take it away Mack!'

Alan stopped and turned his head to the CD player. Had he heard Hugh saying Gypsy Girl?

The song continued:

You do something to me,

Something that simply mystifies me.

Tell me, why should it be

You have the power to hypnotise me?

Let me live 'neath your spell,

Do do that voodoo that you do so well

For you do something to me that nobody else could do.

He strides over and presses the repeat button, standing still while he listens to the track again. Yes, there's no mistaking it, Hugh has dedicated the song to 'a certain Gypsy Girl I know.'

As the song plays through, Alan lunges at the discarded CD case and turns it over. He pulls out the insert and looks at the credits list. There is an * marked in biro against the song. The credits state 'by Cole Porter from the show Fifty Million Frenchmen.'

As the next track 'The Summer Knows' begins, he sits down in Simone's armchair, drops the case to the floor and holds his head in his hands, moving his fingers up and down his temples quickly in an effort to calm the stabbing headache that has suddenly come on. After a few frozen moments another list forms in his mind:

No support after the partners' betrayal

Finlay's secret

Lunch with Jack

Given up on making love

Graveyard with Hugh

Touching legs

Gypsy Girl. . . Gypsy Girl . . . Gypsy Girl

Hugh ... Simone . . . Hugh and Simone. It has to be real. She's deceived him. Hugh's deceived him. When? How? Why? What does this mean? What *does* it mean for him, for her, for me, for all of us?

After a while he rises, and leaves the studio, remembering to lock the door behind him. He walks slowly towards the house. Before he reaches the back porch he looks up and considers the size and shape of it.

All my hard work; the daily slog; I did everything for her and Luc.

Risk of toxicity

Later that afternoon

As he tidied away the semi-sorted bundles of photos and papers into boxes, Alan mentally rehearsed possible openers.

'Simone. Sit down and listen to me please. I have something to say.'

Or maybe:

'Simone, I've decided to go straight to France – and this is why.'

How about:

'Sit down Simone and don't move till you've heard me out!'

Or simply:

'It's over Simone. I'm leaving.'

He decided that his preferred strategy would be systematic, detailed and cold. Gaining her undivided attention, presenting the facts and his inevitable conclusions, and stating what he planned to do next. There was nothing she could say that would change his mind.

In the end all plans were roughly and quickly superseded by his spontaneous reaction to her very first words as she walked through the door with a John Lewis bag which she handed straight to him, with a 'a new beret for you, Alain. When in France and all that.'

'Oh, I'm glad you gave *me* some thought, Simone. Not too busy with Jack today? Or was it Tom, Dick or Harry this time?'

'Alain, what on earth…?'

'Seems Jack isn't the only one. And certainly not the first.'

In apparent exasperation she replied, 'I have no idea what you are talking about, Alain. No idea.'

'Oh really? Then let me take you back through the years, my gypsy girl. Or were you ever 'my' gypsy girl? We'll come to that. Sit down.' He pushed her into the adjacent dining chair.

He pulled his chair nearer to Simone's, leaned in closer than was comfortable for her, and fixed his eyes on her face. 'It seems you really have been hiding things from me, my sweet.

'Jenners sent Jack instead.' He mimicked her girly French accent.

'And as for *poor Hugh.'* His laugh contained a hint of hysteria. 'Just how long has he needed *your support, and a little kindness?'*

Simone felt a little faint. She had to get some air. 'Alain, stop this. Now. Please. I don't know what you're getting at. I don't know what you're talking about.' She made to get up.

He pushed her back down in her seat.

'Let me explain, my love.

'I found this when I was clearing out.' He slid the jazz CD out of a manila envelope. 'Not your usual choice of music I believe?'

Simone made to grab it from him.

'No, I'll keep that for now. I'm sure you're very familiar with its contents. The usual range of jazz standards with one particular favourite . . . Dedicated to one special Gypsy Girl from her cool, sexy lover.' He mimicked the breathy, languid tone of the jazzer.

'Where did you get that?' her breath quickened, the volume of her voice escalated. 'Have you been in my studio? Have you?'

'I've been tidying up – I told you. And that place is a tip!' He held the CD just out of her reach.

'It's mine! I can do what I like in there. Keep out in

future! Just keep out.'

'Future? Future? Oh I think you are missing the point my sweet. I know about you and Hugh. Jack doesn't really matter. Or any of the others. But Hugh? My old buddy? You make me physically sick, both of you.'

'Alain, you really have got this all wrong. First of all you snoop about in my private place, and then you find some old CD from years ago, with a jokey message on it. You shouldn't have been there and you certainly shouldn't be jumping to ridiculous conclusions. Now I'm going to make a cup of coffee. I don't want to hear any more of this nonsense.'

She tries to get up again, but nothing will deflect him now. 'Sit still. Sit there till I've finished.' Alan's tone was menacing. Simone shrank from his jabbing hand and fell back into the chair

'I think I'll make it into a little story, shall I? I might need to fill in a few blanks but I've seen enough French films to do that quite easily.'

'Where shall I begin? Hugh is a suave, handsome consultant. His sexual appetites are legendary amongst his friends. He regularly shags groupies at his jazz concerts, but doesn't normally shit on his own doorstep.'

Alan was standing up now as if addressing an audience. Simone looked on bewildered and increasingly anxious.

'Hugh has a beautiful wife Anne. He shags her as often as she'll let him. She's not very adventurous, but compliant you might say.'

Simone screeched 'Alain! Anne is dead! Stop it! I will not listen to this madness!' and puts her hands over her ears.

He yanked them off. 'Are you listening to me, oh Gypsy girl? It's not *happy ever after* time just yet.'

He pulled the photograph from the Vendée out of the same envelope.

'Hugh occasionally liked a bit of Latin loving. And who better than the lovely Simone? Artistic, free spirited, once beautiful (with emphasis on the 'once') – and very willing. And when better than on their family holidays – sun, sand and secretive sex?'

As Simone tried to snatch the photo from him, it ripped raggedly in two.

'You're having delusions Alain. I won't listen to any more of this.'

He shushed her words with a fingertip to his lips.

'You couldn't really blame them. All day left alone. The smell of magnolia permeating the air. Sun-kissed skin, and the light breeze carrying the hypnotic sound of the lap of distant waves.

'There it started and thereafter when it was possible, it continued. Kenmore, the Scilly Isles, Skye. Fourteen years I make it – and counting.

'Non. Non!' Simone shouted. 'You're wrong.'

'Shut up,' he bawled. 'I WILL finish!

'She even created a beautiful figurine to commemorate their liaisons – the wild *Gypsy Girl* in a state of sheer abandon. Now there for all to marvel at, as soon as you enter the Scott mansion.

'And then when dear Anne tragically died, the doorstep was no longer a barrier. And you know, he really did need support, the poor broken man.'

Alan suddenly crumpled. Sat down heavily, holding his head in his hands, tears pouring down his cheeks.

'How could you do it Simone? I loved you from the day we first met. You were everything I wanted. I never stopped loving you.'

She was crying too now. Sobbing.

'Alain, I'm sorry. I am so sorry. It wasn't like that. It really wasn't. We had an occasional fling, Hugh and I. It meant nothing really. Just a bit of fun for both of us – only three or four times, not 14 years, and it hasn't happened for a long time.'

Alan jumped up, fired again by her words.

'So I'm right! You did do it. A bit of fun you say? A bit of fun? My fucking God. You're my wife. He's my best friend. I've got nothing now. Nothing at all. Gone – everything's gone.'

She tried to comfort him. He pushed her away.

She brought him coffee. He left it untouched.

Eventually he made his way upstairs, and began to fill his holdall with the last minute items on his list.

Simone washed her face in cold water. Sat quietly for a few minutes to attempt to recover her composure and then took the bag with his beret up to their bedroom.

'Alain ...'

'Don't come in. I'm leaving, Simone. Now. For France. I can't stand to be here a moment longer.'

Simone tried pleading with him, tried to hold onto his arm but he shook her off. 'You can't go now. You're not due there for another two weeks. Please Alain. We can sort this out. I love you. Please, stay. I really do love you. I always have.'

And through her tears, 'What about Luc? What are we going to say to him? You can't go without saying goodbye. He has done nothing.' She was shivering, shaking.

He continued checking items off his list, appearing unmoved.

'Wait a bit. Please. Wait for Luc. We'll say you need a break before you start work. Then I promise I'll drive you to the airport and you can go, if that's what you want to do.'

He ignored her request and closed his suitcase with a firm snap, snap. 'There's *one* goodbye I must make. And that's to Hugh. And on this occasion you **won't** be there to support him.'

Chest Pain

That same evening

He picked up his Barbour jacket as he left the house at a run, threw his suitcase and holdall into the boot, jumped into the jeep and slammed it into first gear. He wove his way through the streets of weary Saturday shoppers, bikers and tourists on his crosstown journey to Murrayfield, shoulders hunched, gloved hands gripping the steering wheel, right foot tapping with impatience at every red traffic light.

He reached the road works at Haymarket just missing the green light, and waited and waited. A five minute hiatus which allowed his red mist to turn into cold, white fury.

I'll sort you once and for all, you arrogant, slimy, self-satisfied bastard.

He cursed the Audis, Mercs and Range Rovers which had left not a square inch of parking in the

Gardens, finally abandoning his car with one wheel on the pavement in Murrayfield Terrace. He slammed the driver's door and quickly zipped up his coat against the biting autumn wind. Collar up, head down, arms swinging vigorously, he strode towards the perfect illustration of the difference between the two men – Hugh's archetypal Edinburgh consultant's west end villa.

He kept his finger on the brass bell-push until the hall light came on and he could see through the ornate glass panel, the outline of the man he'd come to detest.

'Christ, Alan. What's the hurry? Come in, come in.'

Alan pushed past him, took the hallway at a run and flung open Hugh's study door, leaving Hugh to try and keep up with him. Scattering papers and journals piled up on the floor, he began to ransack the shelves of the antique bookcase, until he found his quarry – Hugh's recent publication 'Sexuality and the Menopausal Woman'.

'I bet ***she's*** in here!' he screamed. 'I bet I could find her beautiful body laid open for you to enjoy!'

He began ripping pages out of the book, before throwing it in disgust on the polished wooden floor. Avoiding Hugh's restraining arm, he crossed over to the fireplace and a photograph of the four of them at some medical dinner, Hugh's arms around both women.

'You weren't satisfied with one lovely wife were you? You had to have mine as well.'

He stamped on the photograph, before sweeping his hand right across the mantelpiece to dislodge the symbols of a charmed life – silver frames showing graduations and weddings, die cast models of fancy cars, a polished granite stone inscribed with some accolade from his peers.

'Alan, Alan. Stop this! What are you doing? You've got this all wrong.'

Alan grabbed Hugh by his medical school tie and hauled him across the room to the cupboard built into the fireside recess.

'Get the photo albums out,' Alan shouted. He released his hold on Hugh and pushed him round to face the cupboard. 'The France one, the Kenmore one. Do it!'

'What? Alan for God's sake. What are you on about? Let me go, let… me… go..! And we'll talk it through. See if I can help you. Something's obviously gone far wrong.'

Alan drew himself up his five foot ten inches and spoke slowly and deliberately.

'You have been having an affair with my wife – FACT. You have lied to me and made an idiot out of me – FACT. I have found evidence and you will explain to me exactly what you've done – I INSIST.'

Hugh, stalling for time whilst he worked out how on earth to deal with this, went into practitioner mode.

'Now come on, Alan. You've been under a lot of stress recently. Your imagination is running away with you. There is nothing to explain. Nothing at all. It's just you putting two and two together and somehow getting five.

'Sit down and I'll get you a whisky and we'll sort this out. Let's cool this right down. I'll let some air in.'

Hugh moved out of Alan's reach, opened the small side window and then reached over to the drinks trolley to pour two glasses.

Alan leapt after him, knocking the first glass out of his hand and into smithereens on the hard floor.

'DO NOT PATRONISE ME! I know your game Mr Smooth as a fucking new-laid egg. Well not with me, you don't.

'Let me tell YOU how it went. Sit down and listen and don't say a word till I'm finished. Understand?'

Hugh backed away with his hands in the air. 'Okay, okay. We'll talk this through, get the facts straight and sort this out.'

Alan's body stiffened. He pointed his finger at

Hugh with ever-increasing forcefulness as he spelled out his grievances.

'You always liked Simone – right?' He didn't wait for an answer.

'Anne, lovely lady that she was, wasn't exactly a sex kitten, was she?

'So sometimes you strayed, yes? Jazz concerts – disguised as the cool cat Hef. Babe magnet, you said. You couldn't get enough of them, could you?

'But that didn't satisfy you, did it? It was too far from home and too infrequent.'

Hugh was shaking his head, feigning innocence.

'Listen to me when I'm talking to you! And don't act the innocent with me Hugh.

'There was someone closer to home; someone who had your best interests at heart and you took advantage of her. *Poor Hugh, he works so hard. Poor Hugh, now he's lost his wife. Poor Hugh, we need to look after him.* Poor fucking Hugh indeed!'

Alan moved nearer and lowered his voice. 'You knew I had a few problems in recent years and good friend that you are, you seized your opportunity and screwed my wife.'

Hugh changed tack.

'Alan that's ridiculous. We've been friends for years. I'm disgusted that you would think I could do that to you. What do you think I am? Some kind of double crossing low-life?'

Hugh tried to put his arm round his friend. Softened his tone. 'We're pals Alan. We go waaaay back. Don't do this. Don't let these thoughts poison you and destroy our friendship. We can get you some help.'

Alan pushed him into the big leather armchair. 'Sit there and listen. I'm not finished with you yet.

'I'm on my way to France right now. And when I'm there I'll have plenty of time to think about how I'm going to punish you for what you've done to me. You'd better be looking over your shoulder every day of your life from now on. You'd better watch what you eat and what you drink in case there's more than you expect. You'd better think about what you'll do with your life once others find out what you're really like. Because you won't be Mr Great I Am for much longer.

'And as for your precious Gypsy Girl' – Hugh blanched – 'oh yes, you bastard, I found the tape. Have you taken a good look at her recently? Wrinkled and sagging. And that will only get worse.'

Hugh stood up and faced Alan, his extra three inches in height used to maximum effect.

'You're a fucking nutcase Alan. You're a loser, a never was and never will be. Your threats don't worry me. Go to France. I'll always deny everything. You'll never get the better of me.'

He moved to open the door.

'Now piss off or I'll phone the fucking police and get you sectioned.'

'Do what you damn well like. I'm going.'

Alan pushed past him in the doorway

'Bon voyage old pal.' Hugh retorted to Alan's receding back.

'Oh and ...'

Alan stopped in his tracks.

'Je ne regrette rien.'

Alan spun round, lurched towards Hugh and threw a hefty punch which landed smack in the middle of Hugh's chest.

As he made down the hallway for the front door, he caught sight of Simone's figurine, in pride of place on the mahogany hallstand since the exhibition two years before.

'What are YOU looking at? The show's over, *Gypsy Girl*.' And in a final gesture, and with one quick sweep of his right arm, he knocked the statuette off its pedestal, oblivious to Hugh whose last conscious memory was the sound of a loud crash.

Médicins Sans Frontières

Marseille 2012

It's an everyday situation for her.

A bar.

A man.

A drink.

Again and again until demand, or luck, runs out.

Today it's the same bar as yesterday. Bar Caravelle on Rue de la Partigon. Nothing fancy. And it's the same drink as yesterday too – vodka, with just a splash of water. It warms her up, and after a few glasses she begins to feel numb, and that's good, it helps with whatever follows.

But the man sitting opposite her is not the usual punter in this part of the city.

Voulez-vous un autre verre, mademoiselle?

He speaks French with an educated accent.

Oui merci.

She had already noticed, as he poured the first glass, that his hands were clean and soft, not the hands of a Marseille labourer. Gentle hands? Perhaps, but not likely. When was the last time she had such hands on her?

She has been snatching furtive glances at him, avoiding eye contact. She estimates he's in his late fifties. His hands may be young but his face and neck are deeply lined. His shoulders are hunched, he has a look of weariness about him. Good – then it won't take long.

She never feels pity for any of them, the saddos – why should she? But yet, perhaps a twinge for this one; he's carrying some weight on those shoulders for sure, and he was probably handsome at one time.

They drink again, fast, not conversing.

On y va? she asks. Time is money, after all, and they've been there a good half an hour.

He nods his head in agreement, picks up his jacket from the chair-back and follows her out into the darkening street.

The room is sparsely furnished, but clean, with a washbasin in the corner.

She is business-like as normal. Asks him what he

wants, explains the cost of 'extras'.

'Juste déshabiller', he says, 'votre moitié inférieure seulement, s'allonger sur le lit et m'attendre.'

He washes his hands methodically, in the way he's done a thousand times before, rubbing the soap all over the palms and backs, and between his fingers, letting the water flow over them until the soap has disappeared. He dries them on the towel next to the sink. His back is still to her. She doesn't see him pull a surgical glove out of his pocket and onto his left hand.

'Soulevez vos genoux, gardez vos pieds joints', he commands softly. 'Cela ne prendra pas longtemps.'

She complies, although she's growing more uneasy by the minute. This is a strange request, why isn't he getting his prick out?

'Ton pantalon', she asks. 'Allez-vous les enlever?'

He appears not to have heard her. Moving to her hip, he says in a quiet voice,

'Maintenant, ouvre tes genoux pour moi et détends-toi. Cela ne fera pas de mal.'

His left hand slides up into her and his right presses down on her thin, white, belly, palpating it firmly.

'Arrêtez-vous monstre!'

Initially she attempts to pull away, but they're locked up like dogs mating so realises she'll hurt herself if she continues to struggle

He says nothing, simply withdraws his hand, pulls off the glove, walks to the waste basket and drops it in.

She pulls her skirt on frantically, as fast as her shaking arms will allow.

'Sortez! Je ne veux pas de ton argent. Juste aller. À présent!'

As if she doesn't exist, he walks slowly to the door, and leaves, not bothering to close it on the way out.

Shaken, but not so badly that she can't rush after him, she shuts the door firmly and slips the bolt. Leaning against the door she breathes shallow and fast, adrenaline flooding her body.

Another fucking weirdo. Why me?

She slumps heavily onto the bed, rubs her hands over her face and pushes her hair back over her head, then presses her fingers against her eyeballs in an effort to stem the tears that have welled up in her eyes.

She really can't stand this job much longer. That's an hour gone already and nothing to show for it except an ache between her legs. She must get back to work. Walk the street again, find another man, a normal one this time. Ten minutes, give her the money and go.

Case Review

Musselburgh 2013

I often used to think I was adopted, for all sorts of reasons, but mainly because I just didn't 'get' my parents. Sometimes they wouldn't leave me alone – Luc don't do that, Luc stop day dreaming. Always going on at me for stupid things, and insisting I went places with them when I didn't want to go. Prying into my diaries, that kind of stuff. At other times they were so busy doing their own thing that they seemed to forget I even existed.

I went through a phase of praying to God, not that I really believed in him but it was worth a shot – praying for it to be true – that I was adopted. That my real father would turn out to be Finlay, or even, at a push, old Uncle Hugh, and then I could have lived somewhere else, had more company. But simply on the basis of physical appearance I couldn't keep up the pretence. There's no mistaking whose child I am with this bloody curly hair for which I've been teased all my life, my short legs and thick shoulders. The French ancestors both sides have left their mark on me as one of their own and that's never going to change, is it?

Does my father love me? I can't tell you for certain. He's not the sort to wear his heart on his sleeve. Pretty repressed character you might say, at least, until recently. No-one could have predicted that he'd leave us.

I do know that Simone loves me, in her own peculiar way. She told me a few years ago in a rare display of honesty that she'd desperately wanted a baby; but that once I'd arrived she hadn't known what to do with me. My parents originally wanted four kids, she said, but I was so exhausting and demanding I'd put them off wanting any more. So it seems it's my fault I haven't got any brothers or sisters. One more thing I get the blame for eh?

But if I could have chosen my own brother it would have been Finlay, only a younger version. If anyone understood me as a child, appreciated me for who I was, genuinely enjoyed having me around – it was him. And in this recent awful, crappy time we've been through, he's been there for me as always, whenever, whatever. He *is* my soul brother as far as I'm concerned. The timing just got a bit mixed up that's all, the genes downloaded to the wrong womb.

It has been a pretty shit time, I can't deny. I nearly lost the plot with Simone a few weeks ago, wanted to shake her so hard, get her to wake up from the stupor she's sunken into. She wasn't even dressed – at midday – she had a fag in one hand and a drink in the other. I made her cry with my shouting; I was sorry about that, but I thought it was worth a try to see if I could shock her out it. Truth is nothing I can do or say is making any difference. It upsets me to see her like this and I'm out of my depth – she needs professional help.

I phoned Finlay afterwards and asked him what I should do. He said, 'speak to a good doctor.'

I said, 'maybe, but I've had enough of doctors, haven't you?' We both laughed at that. Not nice, I know, but like, you've got to find something funny in all this or you'd go fucking crazy wouldn't you? Just like they've done. When we stopped laughing I asked him how he was doing. He'd looked so awful at Uncle Hugh's funeral, and with all that terrible media invasion afterwards I've been worried ever since that he's gonna get ill.

He said, 'to tell you the truth, not great Luc, and it's a bugger having the case still open – I can't get closure. But once you're dead you're dead, so to speak, and life must go on for everyone else, so I need to get on with mine now. I'm going back to Africa soon, where I'm needed.' Finlay's never held back on the truth, it's just his way, and I don't like him any the less for what he said.

It was awkward though when he asked me if I'd

heard from my father. I hope he didn't pick up on the hesitation. I lied and said 'No'. I'll tell him the truth someday, when I can. But not now, because I can't – I daren't – I made a promise to my Dad and if I break it, I'm not sure I'll ever see him again. He might be a sad old git, and I know he shouldn't have walked out on me and Simone like he did for no reason. But I want to keep the door open with him, until I get chance to get away to visit without Simone suspecting what I'm up to.

It'll be easy enough if I just wait a few months. Then take a long weekend or something. He said he'd send me money for a return ticket and I didn't say no – I've got little enough as a student as it is. I told him to send it to a friend's house for me – that way there'd be no questions asked here.

I have to go, don't I? Even though it's gonna be tough. I have to find out if he's okay. Catch up. See if he'll tell me face-to-face why he left his life and ask if he'll ever come back. I couldn't get anything much out of him when he phoned. He was pretty cagey, sounded a bit weird. Still my Dad, but his voice was like, tired and weak.

Anyway, the old Français will come in very handy down in Marseilles. I've never been there before. Funny really seeing as how Simone was born not far away. I believe that we've still got relatives round and about there. Maybe I'll find some.

ACKNOWLEDGEMENTS

The authors would like to thank readers of Eight of Cups whose constant requests for 'your next book' have sustained them when life has got in the way of progress.

Without the internet, the 450 miles distance between the two authors might have been more than a step too far. Thank you Vinton Cerf and Bob Kahn.

Bill Cameron suggested amendments to Elaine's pretty good French to match it more to the vernacular.

Fiona Fraser brought her graphic design skills to bear on our cover concept.

Both sets of family continued to encourage and support as they have always done.

Introducing the authors

Mirren Jones is the pseudonym for the writing partnership of Scot Marion Duffy and Elaine Atkins who is Welsh. They have been friends and writing partners for 20 years. Now living in their respective countries 450 miles apart, they have somehow managed, with very few face-to-face meetings, to write this, their second novel. A third - the sequel to first novel 'Eight of Cups' - is in the pipeline.

They met in 1997 at the University of Dundee Medical School where they were engaged in teaching, facilitation and research involving all GP practices in Tayside and many others across Scotland. Elaine then became Head of Organisational Development in NHS Fife where she worked with both hospital and primary care clinical and non-clinical staff to improve service delivery. Marion meanwhile took up post as Manager in Alyth Medical Practice, where she guided the modernisation of systems and procedures fit for the new millennium. Having returned more than once over the years to provide management support, she has only recently properly retired and become simply a patient.

Both have three grown up children and one grandchild, and Marion (still married) also has a great-grandchild. They are circumspect about their ages but they can assure their readers that they look much younger than they are!

The *inspiration* for their contemporary novels comes from life experience, places they have worked, their hobbies (from horse-riding to Elvis fan), and people they have met. Story-lines however, are mainly fiction!

Please contact us with your feedback on this novel by visiting www.mirrenjones.co.uk

Printed in Poland
by Amazon Fulfillment
Poland Sp. z o.o., Wrocław